Praise for *The First Sunday in September*

'*The First Sunday in September* really is quite an achievement. It has hurling at its heart but the game stands as a fulcrum around which the stories act and the stories are vibrant and authentic, brimming with the intensity and the desire and the triumphs and failures that make sporting occasions such a sublime allegory for our human condition. I enjoyed it immensely.'

Donal Ryan

'Imagine Raymond Carver meets Donal Ryan and you have Tadhg Coakley's novel. His writing is taut and vivid, his voice compelling and compassionate. From the ordinary experiences of a single day, he evokes an entire complex world. A stirring new voice in Irish fiction.'

Mary Morrissy

'Inventive, polyphonic, compelling: Coakley's Irish chorus lifts off the page to cry out its fears and desires. A visceral sports novel, and yet so tender.'

Danny Denton

'Tadhg Coakley deftly captures those moments when a life, like a sliotar, appears to hang suspended, mid-air, and nobody can be sure what will happen when it drops.'

Danielle McLaughlin

'*The First Sunday in September* takes us through the turnstiles of a sporting event but also into the hearts and minds of a medley of characters who sometimes win but often lose, and whose experiences of life ring true.'

Madeleine D'Arcy

The First Sunday in September

Tadhg Coakley

MERCIER PRESS

IRISH PUBLISHER - IRISH STORY

MERCIER PRESS

Cork

www.mercierpress.ie

© Tadhg Coakley, 2018

ISBN: 978 1 78117 567 5

10 9 8 7 6 5 4 3 2 1

A CIP record for this title is available from the British Library

Printed and bound in the EU.

For Ciara

And from that day forth, everything was as it were changed and appeared in a different light to him.

Nikolai Gogol, *The Overcoat*

CONTENTS

The Traitor

Sean Culloty and Dinny Young lingered for a moment at the doorway of the nursing home bedroom to which they had been summoned. Sean glanced down the corridor. A tiny old woman in a dressing gown shuffled away from him, her head stooped over her walking aid. A nurse walked beside her, offering encouragement. From what Sean could see over Dinny's shoulder, the dimly lit room was small and neat, with a narrow wardrobe, a chest of drawers and a semi-obscured bed. A St Brigid's Cross hung on the wall to the left over two cushioned chairs.

A gravelly voice rose up from inside.

'I'm not asleep, you know.'

A bedside light switched on as they entered the room. The old man lay on the bed, a turkey neck and loose-skinned bony forearms sticking out from under pale-blue pyjamas. He had thick hands, his fingers bent and splintered with old scars and nicks. His head was huge, appearing far too big for somebody with such a skinny frame. His hair was white, as were his eyebrows, which stuck out above penetrating and searching eyes.

Sean stayed back, but Dinny went right up to the bed. He held out his hand and said: 'How are you, Bill? You're looking well.' His North Cork accent seemed to echo around the walls of the small room.

'I'm not deaf,' the old man said.

Dinny – whom Sean and the other players always addressed as 'Coach' – had forewarned Sean that the man was not inclined to take prisoners. 'I know it's probably a long shot, but the message was that he might have the winning of it for us,' Dinny had said, the night before.

'Oh yeah?' Sean had replied, unconvinced. He regretted it when he saw Dinny's eyes go cold.

'He was something else, Sean. There's nobody with his track record. And with the final in two weeks, I don't think we can afford to turn down the possibility of any edge, any marginal gain. Do you?'

'No, no,' Sean had said. 'Course not.' He knew better than to argue when Dinny hardened his expression and tone of voice to steel. He'd heard the name, too, of course. Who hadn't in Cork? But he still looked it up on his phone.

Bill 'Boxer' Barrett (born 21 October 1925) is a retired inter-county hurler and manager from the Blackrock National Hurling Club in Cork. He is most famous for winning five senior All-Ireland hurling medals with Cork in the 1940s and 1950s and going on to manage the team for a period of fifteen years, when Cork were successful on eight occasions. He was most noted for his attention to detail, his unique motivational skills and knowledge of the game.

Sean leaned over the bed, proffered his hand and introduced himself. He felt the old man assess him.

'Help me up, there,' Bill said, and reached out his arms. Sean lifted him – it was like picking up a small child. Once upright, the old man readjusted the pillows and duvet and said: 'Pass me over that cardigan there. And pull over those chairs and come in close; I don't want to be shouting. Close the door.' His voice was somewhere between a growl and the sound of a JCB claw scraping rock.

'Now,' he said, 'ye're probably wondering why I called ye in.' He cleared his throat and took a shaky sip from a glass of water on the bedside locker. Sean noticed Dinny shrug, like it was the furthest thing from his mind.

Sean was uncomfortable with the nearness of the other two men and the closed door. This whole situation felt strange; everything seemed compressed. His knees stuck out from the small chair and touched the bed. There was a smell in the room, that musty, stale smell he remembered from his grandparents' house outside Watergrasshill. Especially near the end, after Granny Frances had died and Grandad Mick was so old. He'd always hated going there with his mother.

'Fact of the matter is that I have something very important to tell ye both, and ye have to do something about it,' Bill said with a stern expression.

'Right,' said Dinny.

The old man appeared to gather his thoughts as he tapped his forefinger against his lips. Then he looked up and glared at them, real venom in his eyes, like they were dirt the dog had dragged in.

'First off, what happened ye last Sunday when ye gave away a seven-point lead to a bunch of red-useless hurlers who weren't related to a team? Hah?'

No answer.

'Why weren't ye paying attention, letting Dublin – Dublin! – put it up to ye and nearly beat ye?'

Some spit had dribbled from his mouth onto his chin and he clenched his hands in his lap. A blood vessel had risen up on his neck.

'Well, captain?' he said, staring at Sean.

Sean blinked. He really didn't need this shit.

'I think the reason is this,' Bill said, his eyes holding Sean's. 'Number one: ye know it all, or think ye do. Number two: ye just didn't care enough. Ye were thinking: "Sure we're in the final now, we're seven points up – we'll get a few more scores and that'll see us home." Ye were thinking: "We'll be fine, they're not much good, sure so what if they get a bit closer?" Ye were thinking when ye should have been doing and if ye cared enough ye would have. And you have to get this through to your players, captain. You too, Dinny. All those players have to care about their county and their teammates so much that they'll die – die for them out there in a couple of weeks' time. There's no other way.'

Bill began to wheeze and then cough violently. He leaned forward and convulsed in time with the wet, barking hacks that were discharging from his mouth. Sean watched in alarm. Dinny rose and tapped Bill's bony back, gently at first, then forcefully, until the coughing eased and a gnarled hand pointed at the glass of water on the locker. Dinny gave him the glass. Sean realised that, sitting closer to Bill, he should have been the one to attend to him. His resentment grew; he was angry now that he had agreed to visit this stupid, bitter old man. They had nothing to learn from his cliché-ridden ranting and Sean could have been at home with Aoife, resting up or doing a bit of prehab, with a crucial training session ahead of him the following evening.

'Bloody chest,' Bill said. 'Pass me that yoke there.' He nodded to the inhaler on the bedside locker. Sean gave it to him, taking the glass and setting it back down. Bill puffed the inhaler twice.

'You know,' he said to Sean as he put the inhaler down on the duvet. 'You know you don't own that jersey?'

'I know that,' Sean said, hiding his annoyance. He wondered if this stuff had really worked back in the day.

'You have it for one year and that's all,' Bill said, and took another few breaths. 'And better men had it before you and better men will have it after you and, by Jesus, if you disgrace that jersey and those men.

'And that goes for you too, Dinny. I know your players are skilful and fit – I can see that. But if they think that fitness, or skill, wins an All-Ireland, they'd be wrong. They'd be very wrong because what they need most of all is heart.' He pointed to his chest and hit it a couple of thumps. 'They have to have the will to win and it has to be so strong that losing is impossible. Completely impossible, not going to happen, no way. Willpower, spirit, heart, backbone, guts – that's what'll win it for ye. And if ye don't have it, that's what'll lose it for ye. Oh, ye need the rest of it too, but without that, you're wasting your time. You might as well forget it.'

His eyes moved back and forth between Sean and Dinny, as if he were trying to decide which of them was more contemptuous.

'Ye'll have to be tough, and by tough I don't mean the fella who hits his marker off the ball and gets sent off. I'm talking about the fella getting the belts and coming back for more. Laughing at them – that's tough. The fella who'll put his hand up, get a slap and put it up again the next time. The fella who'll go for the pick even when he knows he's going to be cleaned out but he'll do it for the free, he'll do it for his team. That's tough.'

Sean fought an urge to look at the time on his phone. He didn't want to leave it too late before he ate his pasta.

'While I think of it, Dinny, will ye ever get rid of those short puck-outs? I don't care how good young Malone is. Lob the ball down to Shaughnessy and he'll win his share of them.'

Dinny nodded and smiled at him.

The old man grunted. 'Now,' he said, 'I'm not pointing fingers at ye two, but the fact of the matter is that there's a traitor in the camp and ye have to find him and weed him out.'

A heavy quiet enveloped the room. It deepened the air, made it seem thick and cloying. The rasping of the old man's breathing accentuated it.

'Dinny?' he said. 'Sean? Somebody is going to betray ye on the seventh of September. And ye have to find out who. Ye have to do it now, before it's too late. The man who's going to stab his teammates in the back. The traitor, ye have to find the traitor.'

He held up his hands and stopped. He closed his eyes and tried to steady himself. He'd begun to shake and spasm in an effort to repress another coughing fit. A low humming came from his mouth. Sean turned to Dinny and lifted his eyebrows. Dinny shook his head, no.

Bill pointed to a drawer in the locker.

'There's a clean handkerchief in there, will you take it out for me like a good man?' he said to Sean. He wiped his forehead and neck with it and pushed it into the breast pocket of the pyjamas.

'I have a question for the both of ye now and I want ye to ask everyone in the whole group this question too. How many are there, these days, Dinny? Including selectors and everyone?'

'Fifty-eight, Bill,' Dinny said.

'Lord God,' Bill said. 'Anyway, I want you both to think about this. Before you answer I want you to think about it very carefully.' He was holding up a finger in warning. He put his baleful eyes on Sean and said, 'What I want to know is this. Sean, are you the traitor?'

'No!' Sean said, almost gasping the word out.

The old man nodded, his forehead furrowed.

'Dinny? Are you the traitor?'

'No,' Dinny said. 'I am not.'

The old man sighed. 'Right. Now. That's a start. As far as I'm concerned you've both made a vow here this evening. Not to me, but to each other and to the rest of the group. A vow that you will not let your teammates down. Your county. Cork hurling. Cork hurling!'

His face took on a tightness and he clenched and pumped his fist, his breathing ragged and raw.

'And I believe you,' he said, nodding. 'But you have to ask everybody else in the group that question. They have to look you in the eye and say "no". That's vital. Sean, you ask the players. Dinny, you ask the backroom team.'

Sean noticed the pallor of the old man's skin. Sweat had stained under his arms and a sheen of it slicked his forehead and his neck. The door opened and a nurse walked in holding a small transparent plastic cup containing pills.

'Hello, Bill, time for …' she said, and then stopped mid-stride. She looked at Dinny and Sean, who had stood up and moved back to give her access to the bed. Her mouth opened when she recognised them. 'Oh,' she said. 'Well, it's a bit late for visitors, but ye won't be staying long, will ye?'

'God, no,' Dinny said. 'We'll be leaving shortly.'

'Right,' she said. 'Well. I'll just leave these here so.' She placed the cup on the dresser. 'You should take them soon, Bill, and I'll drop in again in a while. We'll leave the door open; it's not great to have the room so stuffy.' She scrutinised him. 'Are you okay, Bill?'

'I'm fine.'

Bill scowled at her as she left and beckoned Dinny and Sean to come close again. He inhaled and pursed his lips and let a long weary flow of air out his nose. He scrunched up his face as if a bad smell had just entered the room.

'I have to tell ye something. Ye need to know this. It's very important.'

He shook his head from side to side.

'In 1955 we were going for four-in-a-row. We were on a great run; we beat Wexford by three points the year before. We'd a great team. We had Ring and Josie Hartnett and Willie John and we had a fantastic full-back line. Lord God, they were mighty. That year my brother Ted came onto the team too. He was wing-back. We played Wexford again in the final and they were the coming team, they had the Rackards and Nicky O'Donnell and Padge

Keogh. They were very good, but we were getting the better of them until Christy got hurt. He couldn't hold the hurley, his hand was broken and he had to go off with a quarter of an hour to go.'

Sean knew that the old man wasn't seeing them any more; he was looking past them, his face drawn tight. Sean was no longer thinking about the time or his dinner. Something different was happening now, something beyond all the guts and the pride in the jersey rubbish. He leaned forward.

'They came back at us and Nicky Rackard got a goal with ten minutes left and the teams were level. We got a free in front of the goal and I missed it,' he said, and grimaced. 'Wide. From right in front of the goal about thirty yards out. Then I missed another free, a bit further out. Just before the final whistle the ball broke to me in front of the goal only five or six yards out and I was completely loose. All I had to do was hit it past Art Foley and … whatever happened, I took my eye off it and I dropped it and it was cleared. Wexford scored and the ref blew it up.'

He lowered his head.

'We lost by a point.'

With these words Bill appeared cowed, his eyes doleful, almost frightened. All the aggression and certainty had tumbled away, leaving him as exposed and vulnerable as a straggly looking tree in winter. He continued, head downcast.

'Ted broke both his legs in a car crash the following December and he never played again. And he went to his grave six years ago without an All-Ireland medal because of me. Because on that day in 1955 I was the traitor. Me.' He pointed to himself.

'I betrayed my teammates and Christy and Ted, and the whole county, and I have carried that every day since. Every day. That's a lot of days; it's been a long time.' He paused. 'And it's often the first thing that comes into my mind in the morning, when I'm awake in the dark, looking at that wall there,' he said, almost in a whisper, as he nodded to his right.

He pressed his cheeks with his thumb and fingers and rubbed them up and down the skin.

'Close that door there again, Sean, like a good lad,' Bill said. 'Don't mind her.'

Sean did what he was asked and sat back down. There was a long pause.

'The day we closed the coffin on Ted,' Bill said, his voice breaking, 'I had to tell him I was sorry because I couldn't when he was alive. I couldn't. I put my medals in there with him because they never mattered a damn to me after '55, and I'd have given them all up for him to have one of his own.' He pursed his lips and winced.

'Ye don't know this because ye're young, but when ye attend each other's funerals – and ye will – ye'll think about what ye're doing every day now, all the training and everything and what will happen on the pitch in two weeks. And one of those fifty-eight people, or more than one of you, might have to apologise to those men in their coffins.' He met their eyes again and shook his head. 'Dinny. Sean. You don't want that man to be you. By Jesus, you don't. Because that's what I've been doing all these years, and I've nearly buried every last one of them.' He took the handkerchief out of his pocket and wiped his face.

Dinny turned his eyes towards the window. Sean looked down.

'Because you never think about what you won. Dinny, you might already know this, but you don't, Sean. You never think about what you won. You think about what you lost, and when it's gone it's gone, and if you are to blame for that, you have to carry that load. Forever.' He shook his head again from side to side, as though in disbelief. 'And it's a heavy load,' he said, the words coming out viscous and hoarse, bearing such a weight of sorrow it seemed as if he would be crushed under them.

The three of them remained still for several moments in the quiet that followed. Sean picked up the glass of water and offered it to Bill, who looked at it as if he didn't know what it was for. He looked at Sean as if he didn't recognise him. But then he rallied. He inhaled and exhaled a few times, sipped the water and nodded his head and tapped his hand against his thigh.

'Have you a brother at all, Dinny?' Bill said.

Dinny shuddered as if struck and said thickly, 'No, Bill, I don't.'

'Have you, Sean?'

'No,' Sean said, noticing that Dinny's two hands were now clasped tightly between his knees and throbbed with the intensity of the grip. He tried to see Dinny's expression, but his face was turned to the window.

The old man grunted.

'I don't want either of ye or anyone else to be carrying that load but if ye lose that match that's what will happen. It was eleven years before Cork won another All-Ireland in '66 and the same thing could happen to ye. It could. I was hard on ye earlier, but the fact is that Clare will be harder on ye. They'll stand down on yere necks if ye show one bit of weakness, one slip. And ye'll be hard on yereselves too, and that will go on and on for the rest of yere lives. Ye have to find the traitor and get rid of him. Ye have to be pure ruthless. There's winning and losing and nothing else. Nothing.'

He took in another bit of air and let it out. He puffed his inhaler twice. He held up a finger and shook it, but it was to himself this time, not to Dinny or Sean.

'The other side of the story is this. Sean? You and those other players? The only reason I questioned ye is that I know what ye're capable of. I know it; Dinny knows it; we all know it. Not only that. Ye were born to do it. Ye were put on this earth to play in that match and to excel and to drive and drive and drive on until ye win it. Everything about yere lives has a purpose and in a few weeks ye will fulfil that purpose and bring the cup home. I know this. I know it.'

He smiled at Sean, and his face was completely different, lit up, like another man's entirely. It was something to see, his eyes wet again but soft now too, transformed.

'I know it,' he said, in a whisper that went through Sean like a bullet. 'And when that happens, it's glorious.'

Sean smiled in reply. Another quiet filled the room but it was lighter. There was air again.

Dinny stood up and Sean followed his example. Sean could sense an electric ripple of change. Something had happened, though he didn't know what. He wanted to stay, to hear more.

'I'll leave ye to it so,' Bill said from the bed, his eyes now closed.

Dinny and Sean put the chairs back in the corner and left

the room. They walked down the long corridor in silence, side by side.

At the nurse's station a young orderly asked them for a selfie and they smiled and complied but they did not speak to him. A few nurses and some visitors watched them from nearby with a kind of hushed wonder. The reception area was empty and they walked past it and out into the dusk.

The car park was quiet except for the beeping of a truck reversing somewhere at the side of the building. They walked to their cars, which were close by each other.

Sean was confused. He wanted to ask Dinny what had happened, what it meant and what they should do about it. But he didn't know what to say. Dinny held out his hand and Sean shook it.

'Thanks for coming, Sean.'

'No bother, Coach,' Sean said.

'Right, so,' Dinny said. 'I'll see you tomorrow.'

'See you tomorrow,' Sean replied and he sat into his car. He started the engine and put on his seat belt. He took the phone from his jacket pocket and turned off Airplane Mode.

He sought out a number in his contacts – one he had been staring at often in the last few days since he'd finally gotten hold of it. He looked at the name and number for a long moment.

As Sean put the phone down on the passenger seat, he realised that his breathing had quickened. He licked his lips and opened the driver-door window. He took a sip from his water bottle. His eyes were drawn to the entrance of the nursing home, now lit by lamplight. He thought about Bill Barrett inside, lying frail on his bed, looking at the wall on dark mornings and remembering a match he lost over half a century ago. He thought about Ted Barrett, in his grave of six years, somewhere in Cork city, the medals in a small mound beside his body. He imagined the medals still shining there.

He wondered how many hurlers, down through the years, had been put in their graves with their medals. He pictured trembling hands removing the medals from the padding of small black boxes and slipping them into the breast pockets of suits, or down the soft white lining of the coffins. All those hurlers reduced to bone and dust after all this time, in graves all over Ireland, their medals shining a soft light beside them under the earth.

Sean looked out the open window. A crow called from the big trees to his right and another answered. They both took flight and passed low over the car park towards Lough Mahon and the sea. He watched them until they faded away to nothing in the darkening sky.

One Step

Puking your guts up at the start of a long drive to the All-Ireland final is never a good idea. I don't recommend it. I would have done it out the window but when I shouted at Jonno, *after* he wouldn't pull in, that I couldn't open the window – there was some stupid fucking child lock on it – him and Mick ignored me, chatting away to each other, giving out about somebody. They didn't ignore me when I made pure shite of the back of the car outside Bunratty, I can tell you that. They went fair fucking quiet then, until Jonno started shouting and roaring at me. Mick was giggling; he's as thick as a ditch, that fella. He barely scraped a pass in the Junior Cert, and he was out the door of Flannan's like shit off a shovel straight after – he hadn't a pup's chance in the Leaving.

To be honest, I was probably still drunk from last night when I got into the car. Wouldn't have been the first time, says you. Me and Ray had an almighty scourge of drink yesterday. There were two matches on; United were playing Chelsea at one o'clock – that kicked it off. We had a scatter of pints in O'Halloran's and then we went to a party in some house over in Killaloe. There were a lot of women at the party, some hotties off the boats on Lough Derg too, but by that stage I was more interested in their vodka than what was under their miniskirts. I was clane off my nopper, no two ways about it. I done the dog on the drink all week, starting on Wednesday in Limerick – I was fair poisoned by last night. What happened after is no surprise, really.

Anyway, Jonno rocks up to the front door of the flat around half-seven this morning, flags flying out the windows and the boot, blowing the horn like a man in a bad traffic jam caused by women who won't pull out on the road and DRIVE THE FUCK ON. As if I wasn't in enough trouble with the neighbours. He's an awful impatient man, Jonno, always was, and he wasn't in the hale of his health this morning, either. He was cranky as fuck, from start to finish. Mick was like a briar, too. He ran out of fags last night at home so he'd a big puss up on him in the car.

If Jonno hadn't kept blowing the horn and shouting out the window I might have taken a bottle of water or Lucozade Sport or something with me. Maybe even had a cup of tea with a bit of bread and marmalade to settle the stomach, but no. A shower might have helped too, come to think of it, but I forgot to set the alarm.

I think that's why I puked in the car and we only twenty minutes up the road – I'd nothing to soak up the dregs of the drink in my gut. I told him twice I was going to get sick but he was thick with me because I kept him waiting. Fierce stupid thing, not to pull over, when somebody after a feed of drink says to you that they're going to get sick in a car. But that's Jonno, a gowl of the highest order. So 'twas his own fault.

A few weeks ago the Super put me on a month's unpaid leave and fined me two weeks' wages on top of it. You're on your last chance, now, Lonergan, says he, make good use of it, or the force is not the place for you. The big, ugly Kerry bollox – everybody knows what he done to that young girl from Kilmallock, and she only just out of Templemore.

What he didn't know was the money didn't matter a fuck, anyway, because I was after remortgaging the house for fifty grand, so I was rolling in it, and I was only delighted with the month off. After Clare winning the All-Ireland I was planning the mother and father of all piss-ups and then I'd head to Listowel to clean the bookies out there. After that, I'd be back on track. I was going to sort it out with Karen, pay the ESB and the gas arrears, put a bit into the mortgage, take it handy on the beer and the gee-gees, look after Kaylee, go back to work, maybe even play a bit of junior hurling, and clean up my act.

I had it all planned out and everything.

Karen lost the head altogether when the electricity and the gas rang on the same day about the missed payments. She clean flipped. I had a couple of bad months after Cheltenham: I probably shouldn't have gone over there with the lads and I definitely shouldn't have borrowed that money from Hogan. That was a mistake, I grant you that. First off, guards shouldn't owe money to scumbags. Second, guard or no guard, he'd break your fucking leg, or your wife's leg, as soon as look at you – he's as mad as a bag of cats, the same lad.

Not that Karen knew about Hogan, nor ever will, hopefully. But she did know about the four missed payments because the ESB and the gas company rang the home number, the stupid bolloxes, instead of doing what I told them to do which was to ring me on the mobile – I gave them the number specifically for that purpose. Now they might have rang me and left some messages, and I might not have answered or rang them back. But sure the whole thing was only a blip, only a bit of a hiccup, and I'd sort them out as soon as my luck turned. There was no need to ring the bloody landline and tell the wife.

Karen checked the bank account and saw that my wages weren't going into it any more. I was using a different account for that. I told her that I was just diversifying the banking and that TSB had a way better interest rate, anyway, but she didn't see it like that. So she gave me the road. I probably didn't put up much of a fight, to be honest. I might have even been glad to see the back of her nagging.

I know this is disgusting, but there's sick and there's sick, right? Big difference, too. It's one thing eating a bad bit of fish or something out of a chipper like Karen did in Kilkee that day and throwing it up straightaway. It's messy and all bitty and everything but it's still fresh food. But what I puked up in Jonno's car? Ah now. I was after eating it yesterday, or maybe even on Friday, and it was well digested by then, I can tell you that. With a lash of porter and vodka thrown down on top of it and some other kind of shots, and God-only-knows-what in the house after. Not a good mix at all. I made a right dog's dinner of the car, lads – and the amount of the stuff! I couldn't believe it.

When Jonno eventually pulled over – he wasn't worried about stopping on a motorway now, though, was he? – I was able to get some of it off the mat on the floor and he had a couple of old jerseys in a gear bag in the boot that wiped more off the back of the passenger seat. My own jeans were fucking destroyed altogether but I took them off and put on a manky tracksuit bottom that was all covered in dried mud. Got a few beeps off cars on the road for that striptease, I can tell you. Of course cleaning up gave me a bad dose of the retches – the two boys as well. Typical Jonno, he hadn't a drop of water in the car to wipe anything down, or wash out my mouth. He's some tool.

At this stage his face was after going a bit purplish and he was marching up and down by the ditch, roaring like a bull, the big thick. 'You're fucking cleaning up this fucking car, *and* you're fucking paying for a full fucking valet in Shannon tomorrow,' says he, spitting fire. 'Getting the fucking smell of puke out of a fucking car is next to fucking impossible.' He stuck his head in the back door and recoiled. 'Fuck's sake.'

'I told you to pull over. I told you to open the fucking window,' I said back, in between retches. There wasn't much said after that, on the way into Limerick, with all the windows down, and we breathing through our mouths, our lips puckered like young ones looking for kisses.

I wouldn't mind, but when we pulled in to the Maxol at the Ennis Road roundabout, the place was jam-packed with cars stocking up for the journey. Saffron and blue all over the place and lads coming and going, full of the joys. Just what I needed, this morning, and the state of me.

Jonno hopped out and went to the jacks. Or went to queue for the jacks; it looked like a lot of fellas had left home in a hurry. Mick went into the shop for fags. I bought a big bottle of water, a packet of tissues, some wet wipes and a bottle of Dettol spray cleaner, and I went at it. I got some looks in the shop, with the pointy tan shoes and the muddy tracksuit pants, but I stared the fuckers down.

Of course, as I was leaning into the car and spraying and wiping away with the door open, who walks past only Tommy fucking O'Gorman from Sixmilebridge, the self-righteous prick. He stopped and looked at me, like I was dog shit stuck to his shoe, his face all wrinkled up. And the same man all over me like a rash not so long ago. I couldn't get rid of him the night we gave Cork a right good trimming in the League semi-final replay – down in their home patch too. And me after winning man-of-the-match and keeping O'Sullivan scoreless. Anyway, I told the cunt to go fuck himself and I went back to the spraying and wiping. And retching.

I dropped the bottle of Dettol and the wet wipe then, and punched the inside of the door. I hit it a right few digs, nearly took it off the hinges, until the panelling cracked. Jonno and Mick were still chatting in the queue for the jacks, so I went back into the shop and got some glue – they have everything in those garages in fairness, even if they are desperate robbers – and I stuck the bits back together.

I felt a bit better in the car after Limerick, except for the splitting headache and the sore wrist. I was after washing my pants in the garage jacks, gagging away the whole time, but I thought by then that everything that could come up had come up. I was wrong about that too. I had a good shit and that didn't do me any harm, and I settled into the other side of the back seat with my bottles of water and 7up.

And that's when I saw the envelope.

There it was, a little splinter of brown peeping out of the pocket in the back of the passenger seat, exactly in the place where I seen it a few weeks ago, when we went up to the semi-final against Waterford. It was the only picture the family had of Jonno's mam and dad's wedding, and Jonno was supposed to make copies for all his brothers and sisters for the mother's month's mind the following week. He'd obviously forgotten about it. I leaned over slowly and slipped it out of the pocket, keeping it low. The brown envelope was stained with vomit and just as I was about to remove the photo to wipe it, I had another idea. I quietly folded the envelope twice and put it into the pocket of the shitty kaks that Jonno was after giving me.

We came into a lot of traffic outside Portlaoise where the two motorways meet. We were crawling – it looked like those cocky Cork fuckers were coming up in numbers. Probably thought it was going to be a cakewalk. I fucken hate that crowd, I have to tell ye now; they think they're God's gift.

So Jonno loses the rag. Like I said, he hasn't a jot of patience. He got the brainwave to pass on the inside, on the hard shoulder, to make up some ground on the langers. Fuck it, says he, and pulled the car sharp to the left, but he forgot to look in his wing-mirror, so he didn't see the Avensis bombing up behind. The Avensis braked, but too late, hitting us a right slap and slamming my nose against the driver's headrest. I don't like seat belts at the best of times.

In all fairness, the boys from Cratloe in the Avensis took it well, considering it was Jonno's fault out-and-out. Of course it helped that I jumped out of the car screaming blue murder and came the heavy, waving my warrant card around the place and threatening to have the driver put off the road. It probably wasn't a bad thing either that blood was pumping out of my nose – I must have looked a right sight, all the same.

Jonno was in the wrong, no question, but so were they driving up on the inside like that, so 'twas a no-win situation for everybody. We'd have sorted out the whole thing in a few minutes only that a squad car from Roscrea pulled up and a pernickety Tipp sergeant insisted on writing it up. There wasn't hardly any damage to the cars and my nose gets bloody whenever I get a slap. The worst of it was that, after I calmed down a bit and the Cratloe boys backed off, I got another fit of the gawks and these were the bad ones.

Basically your body is a one-way system, right? From the mouth down through the belly and out the hole. And it doesn't like any traffic going the opposite direction. It's bad for business, I suppose. So what happens is that the further down in the gut the stuff is, the harder it is to bring it up. This fair fucking hurt. You think of funny things when you're in physical pain; mostly you just want it to go away. But all I could think about on my hands and knees, there on the side of the road, were the smirking faces of those Cork bastards and they crawling past a few feet away, no doubt enjoying the spectacle. All I had left in me to puke apart from the water and 7up was a bit of dirty orange-looking bile, hardly worth its while coming all the way up, but it did anyway – and good fucking riddance to bad rubbish.

When that was done, I stood back up, wiped my mouth with my sleeve, sat into the car and slammed the door after me. None of the others said anything, including the Tipp sergeant – they knew that much, if they didn't know much else. I opened the car window and spat onto the road. I put some tissues up my nose to try to stop the blood and it worked, but there was no getting the stains off the upholstery and my shirt. I did what I could with the Dettol and the wet wipes and I closed my eyes and tried not to think about the last few years of my life. I tried to get some sleep. I did too, eventually.

We motored on after that and by half-twelve we had stools at the counter in Quinn's on the Drumcondra Road and I was ready for action again. The jeans were nearly dry when I put them on in the jacks – still a bit smelly but better than that stupid tracksuit bottom. I tore up Jonno's mam and dad too and flushed the pieces to fuck down the toilet. I was probably out of order doing that – 'tisn't a bit like me, to tell you the truth, ask anyone. But you know what? The fucker had it coming.

Anyway, now the day was rightly looking up. Nothing like the end of a hangover, and putting another in its place.

When Clare were making their way through the championship the last few years I knew straight away that I wanted them to lose. My own county – and I wanted them to lose. Even to Tipp. Even in the final against Galway last year. Outside, of course, I was shouting 'Up the Banner' with everybody else, but inside

I was hoping the fuckers would get hammered. A desperate terrible thing to admit, but there you have it.

And I couldn't go to matches either. Not a hope. I couldn't go near a pitch; I didn't have the stomach for it. I watched them all in the pub. That's what I was planning today too, before the shit hit the fan.

I had a few quick pints to get things going and they stayed down, no bother at all. Jonno and Mick were in flying form, giving mighty stick altogether to the Cork langers in the pub about the hammering we lashed into them last year and how we were about to repeat the dose.

I was starving after the pints so I went around the corner to a little chipper and horsed down a couple of chicken and chips. Nothing to write home about, but they did the job. Here's another thing: with only a few hours to go before the match, I had a right dose of the jitters. Remember when I said earlier that I remortgaged the house for fifty grand? Well, most of that was already gone. I had to fix up with Hogan, the headcase, for starters, and of course he screwed me with interest, not that he'd even know the meaning of the word, no more than the man on the moon; but he screwed me, anyway, in that shithole of a house of his, on the Island, with his mad-looking brothers in their scanger outfits with their pit-bull terriers and their 'tashes and tattoos. So that was thirteen gone. I had to pay back the brother the five I owed him, too – that's a long story: I don't want to talk about that now. Then I did a stupid thing and blew another ten in Galway, and that was after promising Karen I'd never go back after what happened at the cocaine party last year.

With a few other bits and pieces of eejitry, I looked at the App on the phone one day and saw the balance at only €18,056. So what did I do? What do you think I did? I put fifteen grand on Clare to win the All-Ireland, that's what I did – this was before the semi-final and I got 7/2, to win the bones of 70K. Great odds altogether. I was all set to clean up; the win was guaranteed. Sure with McMahon and the lads flying and Cork in a heap in their back line, there could only be one result. Adding to the winnings with what I'd make in Listowel, 'twas happy days are here again and show me the way to go home.

But a bet's still a bet, even when it's a dead cert, so I was a bit nervy. And if I was in my right mind I probably would have ignored Jimmy Dolan when I saw him in the crowd outside Quinn's on my way back in. But I didn't.

Jimmy is one of Limerick's finest little robbing scangers, and that's saying something – there's strong competition around there, I can tell you that. He's one of my regular parishioners and he knows better than to go to a match in Gaelic Park or Cusack Park where he'd be spotted. The little bollix thought he'd be safe enough up here with the Cork crowd, but the thought made a fool of him. Or me, as it turned out.

I grabbed him by the collar and started dragging him over to a couple of our lads in uniform, who were directing traffic, to lock him up. But when I took a hoult of him, he peeled out of his jacket and shot off up the road like a rocket. He probably had a lash of money and phones on him, even though they often pass on their takings to somebody else. Anyway, I took off after him, like

I wasn't seventeen stone and after two feeds of chicken and chips and after a scourge of drink the day before and a dose of the gawks and me with a bad knee and not after training for two years.

But you know what? When I was sprinting up the road after the bould Jimmy I felt so alive that I started shouting. I was fucking *flying*, lads, and all the Clare and Cork fans cheering me on. I was back! There I was, belting up the road like the clappers in my pointy tan shoes, my smelly jeans, my bloody shirt, letting fly: yahoo, this is the life, boys, up the fucken yard, I have you now, Dolan, ya Limerick cunt ya. I was gaining on the little maggot too. I was.

I might have actually caught him but the next thing I knew I was on the ground in a heap on a bit of grass beside a tree. People gathered around me, leaning over me, saying stuff I couldn't hear, and me looking up at them like a fool, gasping for air like a fish on a boat.

Fact of the matter is that drinking and gambling is great fun. Hard to beat it really, lads, and that's the God's honest truth. When you're on the batter or you've a ton on the nose of a horse, life is fucking mighty. Why do you think people do it if it isn't the bee's knees? Jesus, it costs enough, 'twould want to be. And here's what it does for you: when you're on that high nothing else in the wide earthly world matters a damn. Nothing. The past never happened. You were never dropped off the Clare panel, missing out on an All-Ireland; you didn't do your cruciate, put on four stone, fall out with your club, give the best part of 120 grand of your money to those bastarding bookies; you were never thrown out of your own home, breaking your wife's heart; you were never on the verge of losing your job; you never lost interest in your only child or defaulted on the mortgage that was putting a roof over her head; no, you never fucked up one single thing in all your born days. Now isn't that nice? Isn't it?

There's one drawback. Well, more than one, but the main one is this: while you can forget about your past, you can forget about your future too. The next drink or the next bet is the only future you have and the only one you'll ever want. Nothing else comes close. That's the price you pay, and every last man in the pub and the bookies knows it. Don't tell me they don't – even if they wouldn't admit it in a month of Sundays.

And I don't go in for all this malarkey about drinking or gambling or any of that being a disease. I just don't buy it. That's a cop-out if you ask me. Diabetes is a disease, cancer is a disease, malaria is a disease – something makes you sick and you have to treat it. Drinking is a choice – you either do it or you don't. You don't choose fucking lung cancer, I can guarantee you that, but you do choose to go into the bookies.

There's the bookies, right? Across the road, or whatever. If you don't want to go into it, you won't. If you do want to go into it, you will. And if you want to bet the wages or the farm or the car or whatever, you will. Simple as. It isn't a disease that made you do it. You wanted to do it. Same with the drink. There's the pub, go in or don't – it's up to you. But don't go blaming a disease you caught off your father or your uncle or whoever. Gimme a fucking break.

And going to those meetings and telling your troubles and all the terrible things you done to a bunch of losers and strangers? Sorry, now, no fucking way. Taking the twelve steps to recovery? A load of old shite. There's only one step you have to take – step away from the bookies and the bar. Step into your own life.

Now, you have to keep taking it, I'll grant you that. But 'tis only one step, and it's up to you whether you take it or you don't.

So anyway, they're working away on me, on the side of the Drumcondra Road, doing CPR and all the rest. A young one is on her knees beside me, giving me mouth-to-mouth and pumping away on my chest. Fair play to her, a Cork woman too.

It's quare out, lads. I'm still in my own body, yer wan blowing away into my mouth and pounding on my chest. But I'm outside it too, looking on, kind of above the whole thing. It reminds me of the time I took those acid tabs with that nutter from Armagh at the semi-final against Kilkenny last year.

I think I hear an ambulance in the distance getting closer, but it's all a bit weird, d'ya know?

I do know one thing, that's for sure. I want to live. Fuck it, but I want to live. I don't want to die here on the ground, like a big, fat, useless heap of shit, and all them people looking down at me. I want to see Kaylee grow up, and I want to get back in with the club. Jimmy Daly mentioned to me the other week that they want someone to mind the Under 14s next year and I'd love to give it a go. I'd love to have another baby with Karen, if she'd take me back after what I done to her; she's not the worst, and wouldn't that be something – a little lad for Kaylee to boss around and for me to put a hurley into his hand?

Jesus, that feeling in a dressing room before a Munster final. Where you'd go through the wall to get at the fuckers, there was no need for a door. That's the way I feel now. Christ, but it was mighty. Or waking up the morning after beating Tipp, and me after playing a blinder, my man not even scoring, thinking: 'Wow, that really happened, that was me.' Sore after a few belts, maybe, but with such a sense of purpose running up and down my veins that I could do anything I wanted. Anything.

Lose weight? Piece of piss, I done it before. Step away from the pub and the bookies? You may be fucking sure of it.

And I want Clare to win too. Not because of the bet, I couldn't give two shits about that. I want Clare to win because it's my county, my people, my jersey.

Up the Banner!

Up the Banner!

UP THE BANNER!

This isn't over. It doesn't end here, by Jesus, it doesn't.

No fucken way.

Forever and a Day

Paddy Horgan looks out the passenger window of the Skoda Octavia as the road follows the River Bandon heading towards Innishannon. He is surprised at all the traffic this early but a lot of people will be going to Dublin today, especially to cheer on Liam Óg O'Callaghan, the pride of Kilbrittain.

He checks again for his little blue backpack at his feet, containing his sandwiches, a bottle of water, a few bars of chocolate and two bananas. He's always forgetting things these days. He moves the seat forward to give Cora, who is in the back with Willie, some legroom. The car is spotless; the dash is shiny and smells of polish, but Donie, who is driving, always looked after his cars. Donie is all spruced up too, Paddy notices, sporting a bright-red tie.

The last of the fog on the water fades away as they near the bridge. Rich red early morning sunlight drifts downwards from the tops of the trees, the leaves now softened to a tawny brown. The place always reminds him of Sheila; they used to go for walks on the riverbank.

Paddy and Sheila started going out with each other in 1982, after that disco in Actons in Kinsale. He had just turned twenty-six and was working in the Co-Op. They drove to dances nearly every second night that summer, or to play cards over near Mallow –

Hazelwood. No: The Hazel Tree, that was the place. Sheila was a tasty card player, everybody said it. Singles or partners, it didn't matter a damn. His pride when she'd produce a jack or a five to win the game, last throw. She often had one, just at the right time, however she managed it. There was a local man used to call her 'the deadly *ciotóg*'.

After hurling training, Paddy would pick her up at home. He had a great Corolla at the time, the one he got from that queer hawk in Drimoleague the year before. They'd go for a walk down by the river and take a spin over to Clon to those summer dances in The Fernhill. They used to drive home by Garretstown and park near the strand. If the tide was in, the sound of the waves draped itself around them, in their own sweet world in the back of the Corolla. The softness of her breasts, the wetness of her mouth and the moans gentling out of her: a thing of wonder.

He thought those times would last forever and a day.

When the car crosses the bridge and turns into Innishannon, the low sunlight hits them full on. Himself and Donie pull down their visors.

'God, lads, isn't it great to be heading to Dublin on the first Sunday in September, all the same?' Willie says.

'Oh, 'tis,' Paddy says, though he doesn't want to encourage him. Once Willie starts up there's no stopping him.

'Will we do it, though?' Willie asks, leaning forward and rubbing his hands together. Paddy thinks he can smell drink off him, but he's not sure.

'Faith then, we might,' says Donie as he slows down the car to stop at the lights.

'We'll give it a lash, Willie,' Paddy says. 'We'll give it a right lash.'

'If we can mark yer man, we're halfway there,' Willie says, and he's off. 'D'you know what I think?'

Paddy grimaces.

His bad leg meant he could never hurl himself, but in his early twenties he got roped into looking after the Under 12s. Those training sessions were where he cut his teeth. Bright summer evenings, with swallows sweeping to and fro above the field.

Boys are so keen at that age – they haven't learned to be smart yet. Or at least that's the way they used to be, those days.

'Pull on the ball, Jimmy. That's it. Pull again, you won't hurt it.'

They were desperate for trying to pick up the ball.

'Jesus, but ye're obsessed with picking up the ball. Mickey! Mickey! I don't know what that is, but it isn't related to hurling. Are you going to take it home with you or what? Hit the fecking thing!'

It's where it all began for Liam Óg, too.

'Good catch, Liam Óg O'Callaghan! Now, clear your lines. Good man, let the ball do the work. Now, Jimmy, over the bar. That's it, lads. The ball won't get tired, I keep telling ye. It'll work away all day.'

'What age is Liam Óg, now, Paddy?' Cora says. There is a long tailback at the Bishopstown Roundabout.

'Twenty-five,' he replies, amazed that Cora wouldn't know. But sure what else would you expect from a Skibbereen woman? 'He'll be twenty-six in January.'

'Twenty-five?' Cora says. She thinks about it. 'Jesus, Liam Senior and Carmel must have had him fierce young so.'

'Oh, they did,' Willie says. 'There was a bit of a rush with the wedding. Father O'Donovan from Kilmurry had to be drafted in because Father Mac had shingles.'

Willie is a desperate gossip. He'd go up your hole for news. Small Willie, he is known as, behind his back. Initially, he was called that to differentiate him from tall Willie O'Shea, but of course it stuck. Paddy doesn't like the nickname, and only ever refers to him as Willie.

He often used to wonder what Willie had to say about Sheila going away. The same as what everyone else said, he supposed. Not that it matters now; sure, it's old news.

That Neil Diamond concert in the RDS. The fourteenth of May 1989. He'll never forget the date. Sheila was clean mad about Neil Diamond; she knew the words of every single song. She had booked a room in Jury's in Ballsbridge. She was nursing in the Bons in Cork by then, earning more than he was – a fact that rankled with him.

In hindsight, she'd been tense all night. He should have known something was brewing. She'd been tetchy with him a few times that spring too. Normally, at concerts, she'd be singing along and buzzing afterwards. Not this time, though. They had a couple of drinks at the hotel bar after the short walk from the

RDS. It was quiet for a concert night.

Later, he kissed her and moved against her on the hotel bed, but she stiffened and pulled away. She lay back and looked up at the ceiling.

'I'm thinking about going to England, Paddy.'

'What?' he said. 'You're what?'

She faced him.

'This isn't enough for me. I want to make love to you in my own bed. Our own bed. In our own home. I want us to get married, to have children, the whole thing, but you don't seem to want that.'

'I do. I do, Sheila. We talked about this. I told you I do. And we will.'

'You say that, but when? If you were serious about it, we'd be well married by now. We've been going out for seven years, Paddy. I'm thirty. My time is running out.'

He sighed and rubbed his forehead. 'I just, I can't leave Mammy on her own.'

'I'm not asking you to leave her on her own. We can build a house. A nice new house and she can live with us. Uncle Seamus will give us a site. I can take good care of her, even with my job.'

'I don't want his fucking charity.'

'I'm his niece, Paddy. He has no children of his own. Tim will get the farm; the least I can get is a site. It's not charity.'

'I don't like this kind of blackmail.'

He sat up in the bed and faced away from her. His gut instinct was to get out of the room. To get away. His heart was racing.

'It's not blackmail, Paddy. I want to be with you. All the time. Not just like this, but I can't wait forever. I won't.'

She turned away from him and cried.

Now, enclosed by the dank walls of the Jack Lynch Tunnel, as Willie gives out stink about the County Board again, he tells himself that he'd wanted that too. In truth, he had. If only she'd given him more time. A small bit more time.

There is another tailback at the first toll, near Fermoy. Cora (who doesn't have her glasses on) gives out to Donie for coming too close to the car in front. Donie tenses but he doesn't fight back against the false allegation. There was a good six feet to spare and Paddy would have backed him up if Donie had asked him. He wouldn't dare get involved otherwise.

She isn't the worst, of course, and she was very good to his mother, at the end. You'd have to be happy for Donie too, meeting somebody and getting married at his age. He never gave up hope, in fairness.

But talk about non-stop. And hen-pecked Donie will be sour now until that Topaz forecourt in Cashel, when he can get a cup of tea and a scone into himself. The talk turns to the Clare forward line and how Cillian McMahon is impossible to mark.

'I tell ya. The only man for him is Sean Culloty; he's as cool as a breeze that fella, wherever he got it,' Willie says. 'Did his father hurl at all, Paddy?'

'I heard he was adopted, Willie.'

'Was he so?' Willie says. 'Well, whoever the filly and sire are, I hope there's a few more foals in the stable.'

'Jesus, Willie, you can't say that,' Cora says.

'Why not? Sure we need more fellas like him, don't we?'

'Because you just can't. You can't say things like that any more. Sure you can't, Donie?'

Donie pretends not to hear and adjusts the air conditioning. Cora doesn't approve of air conditioning since she found out it uses up so much diesel, but when there is four in the car on a hot day, sure it's vital. And you can't open the windows on the motorway as it makes a terrible racket.

'Anyway,' Willie says. 'They should definitely put Culloty on yer man.'

'I'd say they will, Willie,' Paddy says. 'Sure young Cashman is too loose altogether, he couldn't mark his own shadow. I still don't know why they dropped Paul S. Wright.'

Of course there's no adoption now, Paddy thinks. All those girls keeping their own children even though they can't look after them and there isn't a father to be seen. And all those poor couples crying out for babies in their big houses. No wonder the prisons are bursting. Of course you can't say that either, these days.

He thought they had made up, the day after the concert, on the drive home. That Sheila had seen sense. But when they stopped for petrol in Josephine's in Urlingford and he came back to the car, he could see that she'd been crying again. As they approached Cork, she grew silent and her responses were monosyllabic.

When he parked the car outside her house on the Curragheen Road, she looked straight ahead in the passenger seat: 'I won't be seeing you again, Paddy. I'm sorry, but ...'

She turned to him and burst into tears. Then she was gone.

His shock transformed itself to temper in an instant. He gripped the steering wheel rigid and stared down the street as she got out of the car. The car boot slammed and he drove out of the city at breakneck speed, very nearly killing himself twice on the way home.

He assumed she'd come around. He phoned and phoned and called to the house in Cork and to her parents' farm above in Rathclaren. Her father, scruffy in old dungarees, leaned against the door of the Passat and said: 'Paddy, boy, she doesn't want to see you.'

'Look, Joe, we had a row, that's all. If I could only have a word.'

Joe shook his head.

'Paddy, she's on the phone every night, crying to her mother. She doesn't want to see you and that's that. I'm not going to say it again.'

Joe stepped back from the car and stared the younger man down. Paddy backed out of the yard, his wheels skidding on the concrete. He never returned.

He heard a few months later that she was going out with one of the Whites from Timoleague. He saw her in The Emerald one Sunday night, after Christmas, but she was with Joe and Mary, so he didn't approach them.

Willie arrived to the house a few days later, and, over a cup of tea, when Paddy's mother had gone to bed, he broke the news that she was gone to London. She'd gotten a big job in a hospital there, apparently.

'Lord save us, all the traffic,' Cora says. They are nearing Port-laoise, at a standstill with the volume of cars after the two motor-ways meet.

'That's the Clare gang now. They'll have a big crowd up today, they're cocksure of themselves,' Willie says.

'Lave 'em at it. They might be in for a surprise,' Paddy says.

'Ha ha de, they might, so,' says Donie, shuffling. He looks in the mirror and changes down the gears to another stop. 'Lads, I wonder will we take the next exit and head over towards Maynooth and in by the M50?'

'No!' Willie and Cora say simultaneously.

'I'd say it won't gain us much,' Paddy says. Donie can't stand traffic at all. 'I think there's a crash up ahead; once we get past that, we'll be moving again.'

They drive slowly past the two crashed cars. One had obviously rear-ended the other. Six sheepish-looking young Clare fans stand beside the cars. A big, heavy-set lad has some kind of towel or tissues pressed against his nose. His shirt is covered in blood and he is wearing old tracksuit pants covered in mud, with long pointy brown shoes. A guard takes notes.

'They won't be in such a rush the next time,' Cora says, tut-tutting.

'At least there will be a next time,' Paddy says, and immedi-ately regrets it. There is a silence. He knows what they are think-ing about.

They are thinking about his younger brother, Denis, who was driving his van on the Bandon Road one night in 1998 after a feed of drink, when he proceeded to wipe out a young couple from Newcestown who had just gotten engaged and were on their way home in their little Toyota Starlet to tell their families. Denis had been arrested at the scene and charged with manslaughter, and was all set to plead guilty and to do his time, until he got off on a technicality because the guards had botched the breathalysing. He went to Australia soon after and never came back. Their mother hardly left the house after that and died three years later, a shadow of the fine, strong woman she had been. She was buried with only one son at her funeral instead of two.

Everybody stopped asking Paddy about Denis after a while, when he let them know that he didn't want to talk about him and never would. He had to tell Jamesie O'Halloran to shut up one night in The Sportsman's Arms. The pained silence that followed and the shock on everyone's face drove him out of the pub.

But now, as he looks out at the wide-open rolling plains of the Curragh, he wonders if Denis is well and what it would be like to talk to him again. They were great pals, once. He wonders if Denis will watch today's game in some Australian pub surrounded by other Irish people. He hopes that he will – that they will both watch the same match and cheer on the same team wearing the blood and bandage.

They pass a Ford Fiesta with little red and white flags clipped onto its front windows. A couple in the front, a boy and girl in the back, all wearing Cork jerseys. The fair-haired woman has turned in the passenger seat and is explaining something to the solemn-looking children. The man grins and watches their rapt expressions in the rear-view mirror.

As Paddy looks at the grin on the face of the man driving the Fiesta, the knowledge seeps its way through him with a bitter familiarity: he hadn't needed more time with Sheila at all. She would have granted him all the time in the world if there had ever been a chance that he'd have found inside himself the courage to step into the unknown with her.

He watches the man in the Fiesta until he can bend his neck no further.

Passion

The Aer Lingus Gold Circle Lounge at Heathrow was, Sarah thought, rather dowdy. They had tried to create a business feel, with little 'secluded' areas for small meetings, but it was completely ineffectual. Nothing like the British Airways lounges she had been in with Conor on his business trips to New York, Hong Kong and Singapore. There was just something special about BA; that touch of class, of glamour, that attention to detail. It wasn't down to bias, because she was English – it was simply a fact.

Of course she didn't mention that to him.

'If you didn't play hurling and it wasn't in your school, why do you love it so much?' she said.

Conor sipped his gin and tonic and contemplated his response. Sarah was drinking a Diet Coke. She was seven weeks pregnant with his baby and she was certain that the weekend would provide the ideal moment to tell him.

'It's difficult to explain,' he said. 'My uncle used to bring me to games. He and my father played for Blackrock, a club in Cork city. Really, though, there's just something about hurling. It draws you in. The skill. The speed of the ball. It's Cork, too, of course.'

He looked at her then with an expression of intensity, of passion. Not unlike the look that precedes sex, or that she had seen on men's faces during sex. When everything is heightened; when their breathing turns to panting and every moment is engorged with the raw need, the hunger.

She could feel herself become aroused and her face flushed with embarrassment. She wondered where the idea had come from. It was probably the hormones – she'd read somewhere that an increased libido occurred during the first trimester. She was trying to adjust, but there was a lot going on. And now this game, her first time in Ireland with Conor, and meeting his parents – she didn't know what to expect. She wasn't used to being nervous and she knew it didn't suit her.

When they checked in to The Marker Hotel in the Docklands area of Dublin, the understated style and quality of the lobby and their suite took her by surprise. The rooms were done in lime and grey, set off by a stunning French lilac carpet. The staff were just as she liked them in hotels: friendly, attentive and competent, but not fawning. The area was so modern and clean – it reminded her of St George's Wharf.

The tall, narrow windows of their bedroom overlooked a plaza and a theatre, which was lit up that night in funky greens and reds. They ate tapas in the balmy Skybar on the roof and watched the sun drift low over the mountains. There was barely a breeze; it was one of those perfect late-summer nights.

Her heart pounded in her chest when they gazed out over the river and he put his arm around her and pointed out the lights of the conference centre and the new bridge. She thought: *now, now, now.* But she lost her nerve at the last moment. She almost wept in the lift going down to their suite when she realised that another opportunity to tell him had passed.

It took her an age to get to sleep amid the usual middle-of-the-night hotel sounds: a toilet flushing, a passing conversation in the hall, a muted TV from the floor above, traffic in the distance, and the dull intermittent buzz from Conor's phone, on silent, receiving emails. She'd been surprised he hadn't wanted sex, and was disappointed when he kissed her, said goodnight and turned away. He fell asleep in seconds. Sore and swollen breasts or not, her sister Natasha had suggested a good time to break the news might be after he'd 'gotten his leg over'. It seemed to be happening less frequently these days, or perhaps she was imagining it.

She used the time to practise her lines.

'How far are you gone?'

'The doctor isn't sure, perhaps four weeks.' A lie, it was closer to eight.

'But how did it happen when you're on the pill?'

'It must have been around the time I had that tummy bug and we went back to my house. Remember? After that play?' Another lie.

'Why didn't you tell me?'

'I was in shock. I had to come to terms with it myself, first. I was waiting for the perfect time.' Mostly true. Mostly.

Sarah had come off the pill in late April, when her prescription ran out. She hadn't planned it. She was too busy to go to the doctor and the days just slipped by. It just sort of happened. Then it felt right. It wasn't because he needed a push, or because she wanted out of her dead-end job in the gallery, or that her clock was ticking and a baby would complete her life. It just happened.

Things just happen, sometimes. In any case, babies are a blessing. Nothing in the slightest to feel guilty about. He'll be delighted to be a father. He may even propose.

Or else he'll want to get rid of it, and her.

She looked up at the ceiling as he slept beside her. She turned on her side to spoon him. She put her hand on his bony hip, and on the rise and fall of his rib cage. The chill certainty that this would be their last night together passed through her with a jolt and she was reminded of the abortion clinic in Waterloo a few months after her mother died, when she'd had her crazy affair with Derek – that thorough shit who had been married to her aunt at the time. It doubled as an STD clinic, and reeked of people who had tumbled through their own wretched lives into a lesser, sordid existence. She remembered her determination as she had walked out its front door that day: never to fall so low again. Never.

She woke up groggy and heavy-hearted. In the shower, it seemed as if her bump had already begun to show. How could that be possible, when at eight weeks the foetus was only the size of a kidney bean? And how could a baby the size of a kidney bean have hands and feet with webbed fingers and toes? How could its eyelids not yet cover its eyes? How tiny are those eyes? How could its breathing tubes extend from its throat to the branches of its lungs? It didn't make any sense. Lungs, on a kidney bean.

Natasha had been like a whale after just three months and the thought of being so fat and awkward dismayed Sarah. She turned her back to the bathroom door then, and, under the flow of the shower, she did let herself cry, hoping to feel better afterwards. It worked. Sort of.

Late in the morning they met with his parents in the hotel foyer. His mother, Maureen, appeared to be quite nervous, her coffee and scone untouched. She barely took a breath between long rambling stories about their summers in Kerry when Conor and his brother were young. She spoke so quickly that Sarah found it quite difficult to understand what she said – her accent was somewhat guttural. Not to mention the distraction of that frightfully gaudy floral dress.

She had a rather worn-down look, a severity around her thin lips that the claret lipstick could not mask. So unlike her own mother, who had been gentle and open, and who had pulled everyone into her soft, warm Italian bosom. Poor Mama, who had pined away after Father dumped her for that bitch nearly half his age, and died at forty-five from bowel cancer. She was only skin and bone at the end – she looked like a famine victim, an ancient travesty of herself.

Conor's father, Alan, was more reserved, his speech measured with an educated tone. He also had a distinct glint in his eye. At one point, she was astonished to realise that he was flirting with her. She turned to Conor and saw him scowling at his father – she hadn't imagined it. Remarkable.

Sarah sensed a strain between the men. They'd hardly glanced at each other, even when they said hello. Conor sat still and watchful during the conversation. She knew that look well, it meant he was on guard.

She noticed a tremor in Alan's hand when he put down his cup. A hesitation in his walk, that rigid expression. It was Parkinson's for sure; she knew it from her uncle, William. But why hadn't Conor told her? Perhaps he had, but surely she would have remembered.

They were so alike. There was no doubt where Conor had gotten his good looks from, but there was a hollowness in the older man's cheeks – the beard couldn't mask it. A wateriness to the eyes.

And yet, he'd flirted with her!

She remembered to tone down her accent, smile a lot, listen keenly, look them in the eye, say little and keep her knees together. All in all, she judged it a success. But how Maureen clearly adored Conor. She had tried to mask her emotion in their parting kiss, but Sarah could see her fight back tears. Surely Maureen would be on her side when the news broke, happy to hear that Conor will be a father, that she, herself, will be a grandmother. Wasn't that every mother's dream?

'It was awfully good to meet your parents, Conor. Your Mum was ever so nice,' she said as they left the hotel to walk to Croke Park. She smiled at him and held his hand.

'Yeah, sorry about Mam's ramblings, she does go on,' he said.

'Not at all. You're certainly the apple of her eye, anyway.'

'Hmm. Sometimes.'

They stopped at traffic lights by the new bridge.

'I thought I saw a shake in your father's hand.'

'Yes, did I tell you he has Parkinson's?' Conor said.

They crossed the road.

'I don't think so. Is it advanced?'

'I think he's had it for a while and said nothing. I noticed it first in June and then Mam told me. Apparently he didn't want anyone to know, and he won't talk about it.'

'I see,' she said, and she glanced at him.

'He's very proud,' Conor said. '*And* he thinks he's God's gift to women, did you notice that?'

She was suddenly on alert; there was something too casual in the way Conor had spoken.

'What?' she said.

'All that stuff about "The English Rose"? Spoofer. He was all over you like a rash,' he said.

'Don't be silly, he was just being friendly.'

'Yeah, right.'

They walked on in silence.

When they turned away from the river the atmosphere changed. A buzz of good humour permeated the streets. Groups of fans wound their way up the hill and luxuriated in the sunshine with their smiling, flushed pink and red faces. There were almost as many girls as boys.

Pockets of laughter drifted out of crowded-looking pubs. She was glad Conor didn't want to go into one – there seemed to be a lot of drinking. She tried to see it all through his eyes, but she felt so out of place. Excluded, like a pagan at a church service.

The people they passed, especially the men, weren't particularly handsome. That was one of the things she liked most about Conor – that he looked more Scandinavian than Irish. Of course, she daren't tell him that. She had never been interested in a man who wasn't at least six-foot tall and Conor was six-two in his socks, with his blue eyes and fair hair and lantern jaw.

Sarah had been surprised when he'd suggested that she travel to Dublin with him for the game. She knew how much it meant to him. He'd already gone home to attend one match with his mates that summer.

She had jumped at the opportunity. It was surely a sign.

'There it is,' Conor said, as they turned the corner of a tree-lined square and saw the towering mass of concrete and metal rise high above the rows of houses.

'Wow,' she said, knowing he wanted her to be impressed.

'Yeah, that's it,' he said. He removed his Tom Ford sunglasses and smiled at her. He took her hand as they walked past the faded elegance of a Georgian terrace.

The next street was run-down and grim; council houses, many of them derelict. Conor had warned her that it wasn't the most salubrious area but Dublin still seemed like a city of such wild contrasts. Nothing was predictable and she resented the un-familiar feelings of being out of place and unsure.

She pulled her Ronny Kobo skirt down a little after she was wolf-whistled at by some beer-bellied men outside a pub. Conor had glared at them but she dragged him on. Then she felt silly – it was already virtually to her knees. The tank top *was* a bit tight but very little seemed to fit her properly these days, and it was the only red one she had. It wasn't really her colour.

Conor had glanced at her when she changed in the room before checkout but he hadn't said anything. He was dazzling, of course, in a red Ermenegildo Zegna cashmere crew knit with chinos. When she asked him if she looked okay he returned a perfunctory 'fine'. She should have pressed him. She really needed to get some new clothes, bras especially.

On a blocked-off street near the stadium, Sarah noticed a blonde girl with blue ribbons in her hair, maybe seven or eight years old, skipping ahead of her parents and an older brother. She wore a light sleeveless blue top and a yellow flowing skirt to her calves. One of her plastic sandals was blue, the other yellow. She swung her little flag from side to side before her, and sang: 'Up Clare, up Clare, up Clare, up Clare, up Clare!'

Sarah's feet hurt – another new sensation. The Valentino pumps had seemed the best option, usually so comfortable. She wasn't wearing bloody runners for the next seven months, that was for sure. She sighed.

'Are you okay?' he asked, trying to make eye contact.

'It's nothing. Really, don't worry, I shan't ruin your day,' she said, and changed the subject. 'Is the atmosphere always so,' she began, and carefully chose her next word, 'pleasant?'

'Always,' he said, with pride. 'Never any problems.' He turned to her. 'Now, it *will* be noisy. Some fellows might get carried away, after the drink, in the heat of the moment, and so on.'

'What? Irishmen drinking? I'm shocked.'

'Hey, you lot are not so bad at it either. In the Premier area it won't be too crowded. But I'll probably get a bit noisy too.' He shrugged. 'Just giving you the heads-up.'

'Fine by me,' she said, and reminded herself again why she

was really there. She didn't do sports, let alone Irish sports. She told herself to buck up.

Her one and only time at Twickenham with James and his friends had been an utter disaster. Despite being tipsy from the champagne in the tent, she had seethed all through the match. Him pleading amnesia that morning, when in fact he'd tried to force himself on her in Charles and Megan's apartment in Richmond the night before. She'd had to jam her knees up into his chest before he got the message that no meant no. He was well aware too that she couldn't shout at him with the others sleeping next door. He'd promptly fallen asleep while she'd fumed through half the night. If she'd had any gumption at all she'd have walked straight out and gotten a taxi home. It had heralded the end, really – a wasted two years. Live and learn.

But the testosterone of those huge men on the pitch butting into each other like goats; the appalling fans braying and swaying and spilling beer; the drunken renditions of 'Swing Low, Sweet Chariot'. She shuddered – surely this would be different?

She thought about the winter night her father had brought her to see Chelsea at Stamford Bridge. She must have been around thirteen. As they queued to enter through a turnstile, a large group of drunken northern football fans were herded past by policemen on horses. The hatred in their eyes, their shaved heads, their vicious chants. She had been so frightened in the grim, dark, hostile shadow of that West London monolith that she'd almost peed herself. Not that she let on, of course – not to Father. 'Hmm. Now is this lip stiff or is it wobbly? Stiff or wobbly, Sarah?' 'Stiff, Father.' 'That's my girl.' If only he knew.

Already she had learned how to please him.

The rigidity in his lined face last February when she'd told him that she was 'seeing' an Irishman. What a silly euphemism, too. For 'seeing', read: 'head-over-heels in love with', 'fucking the brains out of', 'soon to get pregnant by', 'hoping to spend the rest of my life with'.

Of course, Father had been too English to openly disapprove, but the lack of warmth, or even interest, did hurt. She was certain that he'd come round to the idea of an Irish son-in-law as soon as he met Conor. If they ever did meet. Claudia had phoned that Sunday when they were all due to have lunch in Soho with the news that he was 'under the weather' and 'couldn't possibly travel across town in that heat'. Gold-digging bitch.

At the gate their tickets were scanned by a smiling woman in a navy pants suit, as though they were in an airport boarding a plane. She waved them through and pointed out the lifts. Sarah was surprised that there were lifts, and she berated herself. Why not? A well-dressed middle-aged couple shared the lift with them.

Conor nodded to the man, who wore a well-cut suit and tie and expensive-looking shoes. He had keen, intelligent eyes.

'Limerick didn't quite make it this year, Seamus,' Conor said.

'Next year, please God. We've some good players coming up. Ye're Cork anyway by the looks of ye.'

'Yes, Conor Dunlea. Pleased to meet you. This is my girlfriend, Sarah Taylor. Sarah's from London but she's an honorary Cork woman for the day.'

'Seamus Curtain,' the man replied. 'And this is my wife, Finola.'

Sarah shook hands with the tall, elegant woman, who wore a fitted navy and cream two-piece suit, with pearl drop earrings to match. The huge sapphire around her neck looked real.

'Sarah, if there's a more stunning-looking woman in Croke Park today, I'd be shocked,' she said, and smiled as the lift doors opened. 'You're a very lucky young man, Conor. I hope you appreciate that.'

'I do indeed,' he said, and Sarah felt herself blush. What a lovely thing to say.

They walked out into a carpeted reception area with windows along its full length, giving a view onto the vast stadium and the green area at its centre. A match was in progress, though not many paid attention to it. Faint cheers ebbed and flowed from outside as the white ball was struck up and down the pitch. The stadium was still quite empty. The other couple were immediately subsumed into one of the groups of people standing around. A young woman with a tray of drinks approached them.

'Drinks? Madam? Sir?'

Conor took a bottle of Heineken and Sarah a sparkling water.

'Not going to have a drink?' he said.

'It's a bit early. Trying to be good,' she said. 'Maybe later.'

He nodded and they clinked bottle to glass. She looked around and was relieved to see some younger people in jeans.

'Who were that couple?' she said. 'Do you know them?'

'Oh, he's Seamus Curtain,' Conor said. 'He's … well, he's rich. A billionaire, in fact.'

'A billionaire?' she said. But Conor was watching the hurling and did not react.

Her friends used to mock her. Because she'd always gone for the posh ones. The rich ones, who were mostly shits, some of whom had treated her like a common tart before dumping her. But Conor wouldn't do that. Yes, he could be detached, sometimes. She had often waited for him in bars and restaurants, and wondered which Conor she would be spending the night with. If that was the price she'd pay, she told herself, it would be utterly worth it.

She had broached the subject of them living together, but he'd been elusive. Her plan had been to move in with him when her lease was up in December, even before she got pregnant. When they discussed it, he complained that his place was too small – whereas it was anything but. The location at St Katherine's Docks was perfect for work, though she would love to quit when the maternity leave ended. When he got his partnership from the firm, they could buy a house in Kensington or Chelsea, with a nice garden for the little one.

An autumn wedding, perhaps, the following year. A russet and crimson theme with rustic invitations. The Oleg Cassini organza three-quarter-sleeved wedding dress would accentuate her height – she'd have her figure back by then. A marquee in Hampton Court, a civil ceremony in one of the rooms there. Her little niece Rebecca a flower girl, strewing petals; Natasha her maid of honour; a pink ribbon in baby Clara's hair – Clara, called after her mother.

He was so hard to pin down, but the baby would change everything. Now, she just needed to tell him.

The match itself was a blur. The ball seemed to fizz up and down the pitch at random, and Sarah could not keep up with it. The players stood around a lot of the time in pairs, and when the ball came near them they engaged in some kind of frantic wrestling or they chased each other and swung their sticks dangerously.

Conor grew more agitated and distracted as the game progressed. He had been drinking steadily since they arrived. He hardly touched the overcooked food they were served and Sarah ate too much and felt dyspeptic, the beef repeating on her. The noise was horrendous. One fat man near them kept standing up and shouting something about a banner.

Conor tried to explain the rules to her at the beginning and how teams score, goals and points, and the different colour flags held by the men in white coats by the goal, but it was pointless. She couldn't take it in.

His despair shocked her, when Cork seemed destined to lose. He screamed, almost hysterically, at the Cork players and the referee – it was so unlike him. His eyes rigid with a helpless panic, his hand over his mouth. The match appeared to be nearing its end.

Only then did it occur to her. *What if they lost?* If they lost, she couldn't possibly tell him today. Could she? She was running out of time and they were flying home later. How stupid could one be?

He barely noticed when she excused herself to go to the toilet. Such a relief to get away from the tension, the noise, all the shouting. The Ladies was utilitarian, not that it mattered. And mercifully empty. Huge roars reverberated around the walls and she winced, clutching at a toilet roll holder in the cubicle. Her Facebook and Twitter feeds wouldn't connect — it kept telling her there was 'no network available'. She tried to text Natasha — 'message failed'. She tried to phone her but it wouldn't connect. She felt like smashing the useless bloody thing on the tiles at her feet.

'You fool, you bloody fool,' she whispered.

An attendant came in as she was drying her hands and Sarah stared at her as if she were a ghost. She looked at herself in the mirror, at the huge dark bags under her eyes. She had to rummage in her handbag for her compact. Another deafening roar. Women and girls surged into the cubicles behind her.

She was sure that her legs wouldn't carry her back up the steps to her seat. But it had to be now — she couldn't put it off any longer.

The flow of people down the steps buffeted her. She held her Marc Jacobs handbag in front of her for protection. People were so ignorant. She reached their area, which had almost emptied, and Conor was standing with his back to her. Sarah braced herself and took a breath. It had to be now.

She licked her lips, her mouth as dry as powder.

Dúchas

What I want most at this moment is to leave my seat in the stand and walk down the steps and turn right to the bar I passed on the way up. It would be quiet with the match due to begin, and as welcoming as a long-loved dog. I imagine the first taste of the cool stout as it flows from the plastic glass into my mouth – the bliss. I'm not speculating here, it's what I know. I can smell it, savour it: the chill pliancy of the glass in my hand, my thumbprint on the condensation. The black creaminess, the soft, soothing cotton-woolness of it. The unseen roars coming down the concrete steps would carry no threat, as I lean on the bar counter, drink in hand.

I hope you will never long for that type of bliss, Sean. I worry sometimes that I might have passed it on to you. You know the word *dúchas*; you know what it means.

Recovery – to be always in recovery and never recovered. That's where I am, in my own little Limbo. But Limbo is better than Hell, and that's where I used to be, dragging others down with me. I wonder: why am I thinking about this now, of all times? The truth of it is that thoughts like these are rarely far from my mind, but I'm okay with that. Even at my lowest ebb, you know, I always seemed to be able to hold close the idea that I would survive, I would be sober, I would be able to call myself a man, a husband, maybe even a father, again some day.

Will you do one thing for me, Sean? If you ever have a son, don't put a hurley into his hand. For the love of God, just don't. I know it could deprive me of ever seeing my grandson on a pitch, but I'd hate for you ever to have to go through what I'm going through right now.

I look up at the long concrete beams in the Hogan Stand roof over our heads. If I knew their length, depth and curve-ratio I could calculate their structural load capacity.

A herring gull glides by.

I watch the arrays of swaying colours – red and white, saffron and blue. A previously quiet and nondescript woman in the row behind stands up and screams: 'Up the Banner!' A dusting of spittle erupts from her wide-open mouth and drizzles on unnoticing heads below. Others rise, as if in rejoinder, and bellow at the hurlers who now file into two lines behind The Artane Band. I stay sitting, trying to breathe, looking at the wrinkles on the tweed jacket of the Kanturk man in front of me.

Your poor mother this morning. Neither of us slept a wink, of course, and then she was up out of bed early, all go, fussing over my sandwiches, which she proceeded to ruin by putting mayonnaise on the ham instead of mustard. I didn't have the heart to tell her. The state of her at the door, wringing her hands.

'He'll be all right, won't he? Will they win? What if they lose?'

'He'll be fine,' I replied.

Very likely it was a lie. Sport is cruel. Crueller than you can imagine, Sean, though you might just find out today.

I tell myself to breathe and I stand up. I watch the fifteen Corkmen march behind the band as they pass my section of the stand. The noise is apocalyptic. I scrutinise your body language. You are first in the line, as captain, and I see a rangy, dark-skinned, short-haired twenty-eight-year-old; hurley held in your right hand, helmet in the other. You are the spitting image of my brother Johnny when he was your age. You've a languid walk, jaunty it might even seem. Good.

Sean, when your mother and I gave you up for adoption, it broke our hearts. But you have to realise that we were so young. Evelyn was barely seventeen when she fell pregnant, and I'd just turned eighteen. We hadn't a clue. We were in shock; we were ashamed – they made us feel ashamed; we were frightened. Evelyn's father was, well, to call him a vicious dictator would be an understatement. But I should have fought him. I should have. Our only consolation is that Michael and Anne are such good people and that they have reared you so well.

As the teams break away from the band, I wonder if there is an open meeting going on at this very moment, somewhere in the inner city. There usually is. Pat would understand and pick me up later – it wouldn't be the first time. I remember going to one on Dorset Street when I was on vigil with Evelyn when she was due with your sister Roisín in the Rotunda – probably just a half-an-hour's walk from here. *My name is Tim and I'm an alcoholic.* I touch the phone in my top pocket. The App would tell me where to go.

I rise again with all the others and face the flag for the national anthem. The words appear on the big screen. A blonde woman sings from a dais near the sideline. An elderly Corkman on the opposite end of the aisle to me weeps. Veins of tears flow down his hollow, bearded cheeks. He fears it will be his last time; I can see it in his eyes, in the pained passion of his delivery. The song ends in the usual shortened climax and everybody sits as the players move to their positions.

You take your place at left half-back, instead of on the right, where you were selected.

Pat elbows me.

'They put him on McMahon,' he says.

I nod. If only I could breathe.

I was so happy when I found out that you were growing up in Glanmire – the home of Sarsfields – and that Michael was a hurling man. When you were eight, Evelyn did something she shouldn't have. She went to her sister-in-law, who worked in St Margaret's Adoption Society. Somehow, she persuaded Helen to show her your file – how, I'll never know, but I have my suspicions. The truth is, Sean, that Roisín didn't make it. We lost your beautiful baby sister on a hateful day in May, in a cold room in the hospital, and her perfect little eyes were the same shade of blue as the sky directly over you now while the referee readies himself to throw the sliotar in. Your mother was never the same again, and you know, she was younger on that day than you are now. We couldn't have any more children, the doctors made that clear, because of what they called a 'major chromosomal disorder'. How you escaped, they couldn't tell us, but getting pregnant again might have been disastrous for Evelyn. Then, of course, there was only you. But you weren't there either, or only as a kind of shadowy reminder of everything we'd done wrong.

I never really know how I feel about hurling. There are times (and this is definitely one of them) when I hate this crazy game, and I play down the five All-Ireland finals I played in myself and the three I won. But then, for a few hours today, I had been receiving homage from old friends and foes in and around Croke Park. And I feel it is my due, though nobody will ever hear me say it.

I can see a couple of Kilkenny men a few rows down from where I'm sitting: Tommy Brennan and J.J. Heffernan from Ballyhale. In some ways they look just like ordinary middle-aged men out at a match, with their flat caps, bent noses and thinning hair. Sean, they are anything but ordinary, I can tell you that for nothing. The things that they've done, and the things that they know. My only hope is that, after today, you will know some of them too.

I watch your body position as you close down the space created by the movements of McMahon and the other Clare forwards. You've been coached well – Joe Ryan and Dinny Young did a great job with you. Today is really all about temperament and I think yours is just fine. I don't think you're a great loser but as Vince Lombardi said: 'Show me a good loser and I'll show you a loser.' You got that from me.

You probably wouldn't even remember the one and only time we met, in Páirc Uí Rinn, after you had played your first senior game with Sars and we beat ye in the county quarter-final. You just about deigned to shake hands with me when I commiserated with you, coming off the pitch. It was all I had been thinking about that whole day, and for several days before. I do remember that, though I have no recollection of the match itself.

I was in bits afterwards. When I got into my car, my hand shook so much that I could barely put the key in the ignition. I drove straight home, past more than twenty pubs, being talked down by my sponsor, Tom O'Neill. He stayed on the phone for two hours with me – he's a great man. You know, I never told your mother about that. I couldn't.

On the way up here this morning in the car I had a crazy idea. I daydreamed that I'd congratulate you after the match, if we win. That I'd seek you out, walk straight up to you and shake your hand. That I'd hug you, even. That I'd grab you by the shoulders and look into your eyes. As a father should look into his son's eyes, on winning glory. What did I think I'd see there? Or what did I think you'd see? And what would I say? I don't know. I just don't know. I'm not sure what I was thinking. Crazy thoughts. I was thinking crazy thoughts, Sean.

The game is lacklustre, low scoring. The back lines are dominating, not that I care. Two points to one would do me. You are more than holding your own. You haven't conceded a free and McMahon has only one forced shot, which goes wide.

'He's doing fine,' Pat says.

I nod. 'So far. I think they'll move McMahon.'

As if the Clare coach had heard me, Cillian McMahon, his star player, immediately switches with the right corner-forward. You stay at left half-back. That must have been your instruction.

Pat is a man of few words, but they are carefully chosen. He knows about you. I told him in the horrors one night when he drove me home from the garda station. Old Sergeant Morris was very good to me, I must say. He never charged me and he used to phone Pat when I was sober enough to go home. He was great friends with my mother, maybe that's why.

We draw breath at half-time, the game still in the balance. Clare 1–6; Cork 0–7.

'They're holding their own,' Pat says.

'If they can keep out the goals they're in with a right shout,' I say.

'Very low scoring.'

''Tis, then.'

'Crilly is weak under the high ball.'

'Lynch is some handful, he's a monster of a man.'

'Still. Midfield are going well.'

'Yes.'

'Winning a lot of loose ball.'

'They are.'

Clare come out onto the pitch after half-time as if they mean business, building a momentum that gathers power as it flows. They tack on point after point, while Cork manage only a couple of paltry replies. Now the spirit is draining from the Cork fans and I can see it in some of the players' body language too. A tetchiness rising in them. The Clare supporters approach ecstasy, with the end in sight.

You turn the tide, Sean, when you block Mick Lynch, the colossal full-forward, as he seems certain to score a goal. But on the follow-through, when Lynch's hurley catches you full on the side of the head, there is a pained gasp from the crowd. My eyes are drawn to a chocolate sweet wrapper on the ground beneath my feet. It is a dark, bruised shade of purple on the outside and silver on the inside. It is wrinkled at the edges, the way that sweet wrappers are. It isn't Pat's or mine; I don't know who dropped it there.

Three moments wrestle in my mind. Your mother weeping, Roisín lifeless in her arms, the helpless nurses hovering by the bed and me standing there, useless – a useless piece of shit. At the grave as they put the tiny little white box into the ground. Father Cotter splashing holy water over it and me holding up your mother, all the time planning and scheming where I'd get my next drink. That horrible sight a few weeks ago in The Mass Path field, when magpies killed a young rabbit, the little quaking thing squealing under the onslaught of the talons and the beaks, and me standing there watching them tear it to scraps.

Christ Almighty, don't *ever* put a hurley into your son's hand, Sean. Just don't.

There is a strained stillness, a momentary hush. Only when the Cork supporters stir and roar and rise to salute their captain can I look up. The doctor and physio help you to your feet and you take your position for the puck out.

My eyes prick for the first time this day – and I want so badly to stand up and point to you and point to my chest and shout to the whole wide world: *that's my son, that's my son*. Pat lets out a huge sigh and puts his head in his hands. 'Jesus, Mary and Joseph,' he says.

Now, as if some great light-switch has been turned on, the Cork players can see their way to winning. Mark Goggin catches the puck out and three passes later Ray Clarke points. The next puck-out is won again and Darren O'Sullivan stabs home a rebounded save. Cork are level, and the tide cannot be stemmed. Another two points followed by another O'Sullivan goal bring the last few minutes to a frenzied climax.

And we win.

We win, Sean. Our hopes and dreams are risen. We win.

Pat is crying beside me, and laughing. Wiping his eyes with a big old handkerchief. He hugs me – for the first time, I might add. He's not the most tactile.

'Oh, Jesus, oh, sweet Jesus, Tim,' he says, convulsing, into my ear. I hold him tight and avoid meeting his eyes.

So now you know. What it's like to win an All-Ireland. I'll never forget my first – it seemed like all the light of the world shone right down on us that day. That's what you're feeling now. And that's what I'm feeling again now, too. I thank you for that. What I said earlier, about not putting a hurley into your son's hand – I take it back. We need our sons to hurl, Sean, and their sons too.

I watch you jump around the pitch with your comrades. I know you'd have died for them out there today and they for you. That's precious, kid, that's a rare and priceless thing – to feel that bond with other men. Soldiers speak of it in hushed tones. I shake hands with Cork and Clare people as we try to gather our composure. Time means nothing. I feel myself breathe again. I don't think I'll need a meeting after all today but I'll go tomorrow night, in Ballincollig.

I think of Evelyn but I know I won't have reception to phone her for a while. I think of Roisín, how proud she would have been of you and you of her, if you ever did meet. I see her as a musician, somehow, with fine delicate hands and pale skin, in a conservatory in London. I think of my own father and his pride and joy when he lived long enough to see me win my first medal. I'll go to their graves tomorrow.

Your mother has had it tough. Her lowest point was when you were about ten. I was sober at the time, thankfully; otherwise I dread to think what would have happened. I was at work one day when I received a phone call from the guards in Glanmire. She'd been detained there, outside your school. A parent had called them because Evelyn was asking boys your age their names. This led to a long stay in St Patrick's Hospital in Dublin, but she was very lucky to be put into the care of a young psychiatrist from Cavan, Mary Hannon, who did wonders with her. She's good now, I have to say, but I do know that she still wakes up every morning hoping for a letter from Tusla with a tracing request from you. This is her Limbo, Sean, and it's a hard place to live.

After a time, after most of the Clare fans have left the stadium and our euphoria has subsided, a giddy sense of order descends over the place. I watch you and your teammates gather and walk up the hallowed steps to receive the cup.

When you are about halfway there, I notice Michael force his way through the ecstatic Cork fans. He pulls you to him. He kisses you on the cheek. You press your foreheads together. He draws you into his arms and I see all the joy that one man can ever possibly know right there in his tearful eyes.

I turn and begin my walk down through the stadium. At the bar just below our section two Clare men have begun to drown their sorrows and are taking their first greedy sups out of pints of porter. My feet bring me onwards in the stream of people flooding away towards home.

A Corkman tries to engage me in conversation with a comment about how lucky Cork were. I blank him and watch my feet on the concrete steps. A Clare man and his son pass me, moving swiftly. The boy is about eighteen and has the number seven on his jersey. He has the look of a wing-back too, though he's a bit skinny. That's easily fixed. His father turns his head as they pass; he glances at me and I at him and something passes between us.

I imagine you skipping up the last steps to the podium. Grinning. Turning and seeing your teammates in a line below you, Cork fans all around the stadium. I picture Michael, glowing, looking up at you, the touch of your cheek still warm on his lips, the press of your forehead on his forehead. His hands still tingling from the sweat on the short hairs at the nape of your neck.

At the large blue exit gate I look to my left, towards the tunnel entrance where the dressing rooms are, under The Davin Stand. A bored official stands at the opening with a walkie-talkie. It wouldn't be hard to get in there, I've done it before. You and the other players will come out into that tunnel to get on to the bus. People course down Jones' Road outside. John Lynch, from Fermoy, salutes me.

I hear the president of the GAA finish his long meaningless speech over the tannoy before he hands you the cup. I pause. The roars rise to a crescendo as you take it from him and raise it to the sky.

As I fumble for my phone with trembling hands, I hear your exclamation burst through the speakers.

'A Chairde Gael, A Chairde Chorcaíoch!' you shout, but the voice I hear is my own.

Five Seconds

One

Cash is going to hit it long, but you know that, don't you, Sully boy, he's under too much pressure and at this stage with only a few minutes left, he just wants to get the ball away to fuck out of danger, and it will probably go high and wide, and it probably doesn't matter anyway, a wide's as good as a score now, the game's as good as over, you're out the gap, but just in case, you rise up a little on your toes and pivot, because there's some space inside – even after the first goal and even with the end of everything in sight you still want more, fuck yeah, you really want more with a lip-licking want, an eye-widening want, a panting, cock-hardening want, more goals, more points, more punishment for that bullock Quinn and those Clare fuckers who trolled you on Twitter, who jeered you in the first half when you missed that pick; more glory, more fame, more mischief, more knickers being pulled down, more pussies opening up under you soft and wet, more tits, more ass, more women grinning teeth and tongues and lips, more blondes, more brunettes, more redheads, more dark ones, more life, more, more, more moments like this one when the whole world is following your tune, your beat, you're the lead singer, you're the lead guitarist too, you're the whole fucken band and you want more of this, this magic, this top doggery, this ownership – you own this whole team: Malone;

Coughlan, Crilly, O'Callaghan; Culloty, Goggin, Cashman; Keane, Murphy; McCarthy, Shaughnessy, Clifford; O'Shea, O'Sullivan, Clarke, you own every Cork hurler, you own those 82,000 people around you, you own the million people watching, all the Clare losers who hate you in their half-arsed mountainy county, all the people watching, in pubs in Dublin, in pubs in London, on the net in Melbourne, in bars in New York and Chicago, you own them all, you own all the hurlers watching, all the hurlers of the past, of the present, of the future, watching, their eyes all on you, you own the Cork people who love you all over the city in Blackpool and Farranree, and Knocknaheeny and Sundays Well and Bishopstown and Blackrock and Togher and Douglas and Mayfield, you own Cork people all over the county and the world, you own the fucken world now and that ball, that ball, that ball when it gets to you in five seconds you own that ball, it's yours to do whatever you want with it, it's yours and yours alone, that ball, so you get ready to hit the bullock, just a quick sneaky nudge, just as he's turning in case he sees it coming, he's thick but he's not that thick, so instead of getting away from him inside and up to the edge of the square where the action will be, you know it's gonna be there, you know it, instead you turn into him and hit him a shoulder and the bullock isn't expecting it and he's off balance on one foot, so he's gonna land on his arse and the ref is too thick to look ahead, he's still watching Cash who's just hit the ball but you know it's coming, it's coming, and it's yours now for sure and the umpires might or might not have seen it but they won't have the nerve to call it, and they can't stop you, nobody can stop you, and now,

now that ball is yours, you own that ball, you fucking own it – that ball, that ball.

Two

That ball still has eighty-five metres to come but it won't take long, it won't be a long four seconds, really, and if you had paid attention to Mr Cuthbert in maths class you'd probably be able to calculate how long exactly, if it travels at 100 or 200kmph and it has 80 or 85m to come or what-the-fuck-ever, but you didn't and you're not sorry, who the fuck cares, because whatever the speed and whatever the distance, it doesn't matter, it's yours as sure as that job in Seamie's bar in Chicago is yours when you head over there in a couple of weeks and as sure as you'll make it your own and become the manager there, and you'll head to New York city because Seamie will feel threatened when you're around his girlfriend, and you'll manage a bar in The Bronx and then two and then three and you'll buy shares in that place on 115th and Broadway and in a couple of year's time who'll walk in only Kim, yes Kim, this rich, hot, half-Asian chick from California taking classes in Columbia, but you don't know how rich and you won't for a while but here she comes, strolling into your bar like she owns it, all cheeky smile and dark hair, and punk T-shirt and she gives you the look and you know you're in there, so what, like, it wouldn't be the first time, but she comes back on her own a few nights later and this time it's not just banging her brains out, bed hopping all over the floor, you both talk to each other this time, really talk, and she's funny and smart, you don't know how smart yet, and something happens that doesn't ever happen to you, does it, you miss her after a few weeks when she has to go back to Stanford and you look forward to the FaceTimes and when she asks you out there, you jump at the chance and you don't like this feeling of not having control, you're not used to it, but you do like it too and what do you know, you go and fall in love with her and that's that, you're hooked now and that wasn't the plan but there was no plan and everyone has a plan until they get a punch in the face, so ye set up shop and would you believe it, you go and get married – you! married! – and ye have two kids, Mia and Sonny, and nobody is more shocked than you are, you of all people a proper dad, but it seems to work, you keep your shit together and you keep your dick in your pants, which is some achievement running a bar in Oakland, but that job doesn't last long when you learn that Kim isn't just rich, but super-rich, and maybe that had something to do with the wedding and the baby and maybe it didn't but it's going to happen and then it's all a nice tan by the pool, and a nice golf swing and a nice couple of mojitos in the country club after a nice eighteen holes, served by a nice Puerto Rican girl you don't look twice at but, hey, that ball's coming and you better keep your fucken eye on it, so you do, you do, and now that it's gone from Cash's hurley and on its way, you know for sure it's not going to be long and high but on the money and you're not even thinking now, it's all instinct, it's all muscle memory, it's what all the training sessions were for, all the sacrifices, all the nights in watching box sets instead of on the beer with your pals, all the girls you missed out on, all the body fat tests, all the interval workouts, all the fucking whey, all the wet nights in Páirc Uí Rinn getting dog's abuse from Jimmy

Mac, all the injuries and recoveries, all the prehab, all the belts from Liam Óg in training, all the boring yoga, all the lectures from Dinny Young, all the chicken and pasta, all the chicken and pasta, all the, Jesus Christ not again, chicken and pasta, all the S&C reps: press ups, sit ups, squats, tucks, weights, stretches, lunges, planks, burpees, this is what it was all for, and there's a hundred and one things going on at the same time in your whip-crack-smart mind and they all lead to one thing – the catch, the catch, the all-mighty catch.

Three

You pity them, don't ya kid, those poor cunts who never caught a sliotar, and most people haven't, most people have never felt the sting of the rim on their fingers, never judged the heft of its speed, never heard the slap of the leather on their palms, never squeezed their knowing fingers around its smooth-rough skin, you pity them because they haven't lived, not one single day, and they know nothing, absolutely nothing, they haven't lived and they don't even know that, but there's one thing catching a sliotar up in the high field having a puck around with your brother or your dad or your pal and there's another thing doing it in a winter challenge match against The Barrs, but to do it when there's ash flying and hands grasping and bodies shoving and 82,000 people shouting and a million people watching and the fate of the Liam MacCarthy Cup in the balance, when history is being written, and destinies are being fulfilled, and legends are being hammered, cast, forged with an everlasting rigour, and lives are on the cusp, when immortality is literally within reach, where the past and the present and the future meet, just there, right there, well, to do it then or not to do it then, never do it then, never, never – if they don't know that, what *do* they know? They don't know notten, boy, nor ever will, and they need to face up to it, but you know this, don't ya kid, *you* know this, and yet what you don't know as the ball is on its way down now, it's coming down now, nearly there, what you don't know is that when you strike this ball this ball *this* ball to the back of the net, what you don't know is that it will be the last time in your life that you'll ever hit a sliotar with a hurley, imagine that – the very last time, and nobody else knows it either, nobody, not one single person, not your mother watching this moment unfurl at her sister's house in Ballincollig because she was too nervous to come to the game, good old Mam, saying 'catch it, Darren, catch it' between her fingers, surrounded by your screeching cousins and their screeching neighbours, or your father, drunk now, in his local, in The Rock Bar on the Falls Road, drunk now and telling all the disbelieving drinkers around him that's my son, there, aye, that's my Darren, scoring goals for the Rebel County, that's my wee boy, so it is, and Deirdre Cummins in the Hogan Stand doesn't know it's your last puck, Deirdre Cummins, who worships the ground you walk upon, who's pregnant with your son, Gavin, she doesn't know either that you're planning to run away to the US and leave her in the lurch, no, nobody knows it's your last puck, nobody knows, nobody, and so what: it doesn't matter.

Four

It doesn't matter because as sure as the sun will rise up over Cork Harbour and set down over Knocknaheeny tomorrow, this goal is on its way, destiny is here and now, glory glory here it comes, and Ray Clarke does something great, something that you see from the corner of your eye, and you think 'you fucken good thing, Clarkey' and Joe O'Connell, the Clare goalkeeper sees it and there's nothing he can do apart from shout, but Ian Keane, Ray's marker doesn't hear him, so when Ray leaves his place and moves out towards the twenty-one into the middle Ian follows him because he doesn't want *his* man to score, no he doesn't want that, and Ray shouts 'bat it, Darren, bat it', which was the code for catch it and if he shouted 'catch it, Darren' it was code for bat it, and you know the goal is on now but you already knew, and Ian tries to get between you and Ray to get the batted ball, but in doing that he makes the space inside free, which is why Ray did it in the first place, smart Ray, good Ray, sweet Ray, poor Ray who will kill himself, aged forty-two, put a rope around his neck in his garage for his wife, Paula, to find him hanging there, bad Ray breaking his wife's heart, breaking his kids' hearts and fucking up their lives, breaking his mother and father's hearts, but he couldn't help it, he couldn't, all that pain, he just wanted it to stop, but now he's not poor Ray or bad Ray, he's great Ray, because now Ian has come out, the bullock is only getting up off his arse and you're gliding into space, into where the ball will land, and Joe O'Connell in the goal fucks up too because he doesn't come out, he doesn't come out, he stands there and hedges his bets because if he comes out and you get a hurley to it first you might tap it over his head into an empty goal and then it would be all about Joe and he doesn't want that, no he doesn't want that, so he settles on the goal line, small and ineffectual, he settles just like he'll settle for Trish Quinlan instead of really going after Cathy Dempsey, he wanted her, and he settled for the teaching that he will always hate, when all he ever wanted to do was just to play music on his fiddle and maybe to write some too, why not, he hears tunes in his head, he hears them but he drives them away, like he now drives away the thought that if he comes to meet the ball he might save a goal, so it's yours alone and you're drifting in to meet it, and you're arching backwards, eyes on the ball, it's nearly here, and now everyone can see, the whole ground, the whole world can see, they can all see, and you're bracing your knees for the jump, just a small jump and you know that you'll have to, but that's okay, that's fine, so you do, you jump slightly, and reach your long arm out and you lean back and here comes the ball and there you are reaching and millions of eyes are watching and nobody in the world is breathing – everything is moving now to the sound of a different heartbeat, slow and steady, every single thing, as the ball drops like it's coming home, it's home, home forever, sweetly, oh so sweetly home.

Five

The ball sticks to your hand, but only for an instant because in one movement you're landing, you're moving forward, you're gently tossing the ball up, easily, languorously, you're just tossing the ball up, and now all the Cork people are rising off their seats and the Clare people are wincing because everybody knows now, and you're twisting your torso, swinging the hurley back to your left, shortening it slightly in case there'll be a hook but there won't be a hook, and the ball is in the air waiting, just waiting there for time to do its thing and time does its thing and slows itself down to take a good look, so that everyone watching can be in this moment forever, to savour the pain and the pleasure always, and time says okay that's enough and the hurley is at the end of its back-swing and now you're powering it forward, adjusting your feet, bracing your knees, winding up your hips for the hit, and the goalie is tiny, and the ash meets the leather and the ball is flattened where the wood hammers it, and the ball is being driven forward and it's it's it's *it's a long high clearance from Jack Cashman into the Cork full-forward line, only three minutes left in this All-Ireland final, and Darren O'Sullivan is rising, and Sullivan catches and Sullivan strikes and it's a goal, it's a goal, it's a goal for Cork and Darren O'Sullivan, and surely now the Liam MacCarthy Cup is heading to Leeside, with Darren O'Sullivan's second goal here today in Páirc an Chrócaigh and his ninth in this year's Hurling Championship*, and the ball powers into the net and it billows whitely, ball and net, net and ball, and you're turning away, grinning, your arms stretched wide to milk the acclaim of the Cork fans in the Davin Stand for this goal, this goal, this, and you'll think about this goal too many years from now, when your granddaughter, Lee, the first of your three grandchildren, bless them, Mia's eldest girl (Sonny won't have kids), when Lee runs up to you all excited after she finds the little tattered box in one of your drawers in the beach house, where your medal had lain forgotten all this time, to ask you about it, and you sit her up on your lap and show her the video on YouTube, the old video of all your nine goals still there after all this time, and she says: 'Is that you with the stick, Ganda?' and you say, 'Yes, honey', and you make a brooch of your medal and give it to Mia, 'You're half Cork you know', and she'll wear it at your funeral and people will ask what that word is, and she'll say 'it's *Éire*, it means Ireland, it was Pop's, he won it, and that's a harp in the middle, the symbol of Ireland', and she'll wear it again a couple of weeks later when Kim spreads your ashes into the sea, near where you liked to be, towards the end, weak from chemo, walking barefoot by the tide, hand-in-hand with little Lee, who likes to look for shells, and where you like to look out over the water, imagining home, thinking about your childhood, the only child of an unhappy marriage, your father coming and going between shouting matches, growing up tough, not caring, finding freedom in hurling, an escape, finding the game come easy to you, liking the limelight, then loving it, loving the sound in your ears after that goal, that sound, you can still hear that sound, can't you, after all the years, as you wheeled away, arms spread wide, Ray running up to hug you, yes, as you walk the sandy beach hand-in-hand with your perfect little granddaughter, you think about those five seconds, your five seconds,

      waiting for that eternal sliotar,

         falling,

            falling pliantly

               into your upstretched open palm,

                  falling joyfully,

                     forever falling from out of a clear blue
                     September sky.

Áine Laughs

On the way up to Dublin in the car, as she listened to one Joni Mitchell song after another, Áine could no longer deny the sour realisation: that hurling had been her thing and never really Suzie's at all. Perhaps she'd always known, but wanted to ignore it. Like when you get that first tingling of a cold sore and you know it's coming, but you still want to pretend it's a false alarm. Until, that is, it blisters and swells and cracks the skin, breaking open into an ugly crusting scab on your lip for all the world to see.

Baptiste is as stiff and correct as ever as she checks in to The Clarence. She looks around the small lobby, with its wooden panels and deep carpet and those big old doors. So much the same, so different now.

'Hello, Ms O'Keefe. Áine. Very nice to see you again. Up for the match?' he says, noticing the Cork jersey she is wearing. He pronounces it 'ze match'. She had warned him several times to use her first name but it doesn't sit well with his rigorous formality.

'I am indeed, Baptiste, I'm a martyr for it, as we say.' She signs the form, trying to mask the shake in her fingers.

'Your key cards,' he says. 'Room 301, as requested.'

Áine takes one card out of the sleeve and places it on the desk.

'One will do,' she says, meeting his eye. He nods his head to one side and that's as much as she gets. What a handsome man, though.

They'd met him one night in the Front Lounge, and he immersed in a stunning-looking, six-foot-something Viking with a reddish-blond beard. Deep powder-blue eyes. So he'd have no interest, anyway, even if she did, which she doesn't. Suzie never shut up about the blond man all night until Áine got jealous and fell into a sulk.

Luka, the quiet Pole who had always been uncomfortable around herself and Suzie, has brought in her case and stands to attention nearby, the car keys in his hand. She has her €2 coin ready to give him when he brings it up to her room.

Baptiste smiles again and tells her to have a nice stay. Yeah, right. Have a nice stay. On your own, while your 'partner' or 'ex-partner' or whatever-the-hell-she-is-now swans around San Francisco in her new corporate Vice-Presidential $1,200 power suit looking down on the LGBT capital of the US from her swanky penthouse suite.

When Luka turns to leave the bedroom, the €2 coin in his hand, she almost asks him to stay. She stands alone in the room and it seems darker than before. She turns on all the lights. Some music is being played in Temple Bar, she can hear it through the window – a song she doesn't know. She looks at the suitcase on the stand. She goes into the bathroom and runs a bath.

Afterwards, when she has finished her room-service coffee and winced at the bill, she puts on her favourite top – the long blue one they bought together in Chelsea when Suzie had to work in New York and Áine had a free weekend in that posh Central Park hotel. It goes so well with those magical leggings, which somehow manage to make her thighs look reasonable, and those navy Camper wedge pump sandals she got in Malaga. The top has a high neck so she chooses the simple Michael Kors pendant for outside, but her Enibas drop studs will impress even the pickiest of bitches in The George. Everybody loves a classy pair of earrings.

She tries to keep her hand steady as she applies lipstick and thinks of Suzie dressing up, as only she can, putting on something lacy, a short skirt, going out to some fancy place on a hot date with an impossibly beautiful and accomplished gym-toned American blonde.

She goes down to the Octagon Bar before dinner. They have Bombay Sapphire and it tastes like nectar. So she has a second one. But the moment she sits into the taxi she knows that she's made a mistake. What the hell had she been thinking? What kind of a fool does this to herself? The driver tries to engage her in conversation. He's heard it is a good restaurant. Is she up for the weekend? Traffic is very bad because of all the buses. The government hasn't a clue. She tries to be pleasant and make the right noises until she remembers what she's up to and can't be bothered any more. Her phone shows three messages, six missed calls, eight notifications on Facebook. She twiddles with the gold band on her wedding finger. Her late mother's, which she wears from time to time. When the car pulls up outside the restaurant, she almost baulks. How easy it would be to just turn around and eat in the hotel. She closes her eyes, opens them again and takes some money from her bag.

A different headwaiter greets her at the restaurant; Miles

must have taken the weekend off. Áine is disappointed; she was all set for a reaction from Miles, some understated sympathy – a look of understanding. The new person is a woman; she puts her at forty-five. Good-looking, maybe South African, she wears her hair in a bun and needs to get a suit another size up, or lose a kilo or two. But the smile isn't too fake, the make-up looks expensive and those brown eyes! God, they are huge. She wears an engagement ring, a massive rock. A thick golden band beside it. Well-manicured ivory nails against sallow skin.

'Good evening. Welcome to Chapter One.'

'Hi, my name is Áine O'Keefe and I've booked a table for two.'

'Ah yes, welcome, here you are. I have you near the back. Nice quiet table.'

She leads Áine down the dim corridor and to the right, into the arched area, past some other tables on both sides. It's early, so just a few couples and one group of tourists are eating. Her table is at the end, in a central position. She will be on display there. Damn.

'Ah,' Áine says. 'Would any of these be available?' She points right and left. 'You see, I have a little problem. I'm actually on my own, the other person couldn't make it tonight.'

'That's no problem at all. Will here be okay?' the headwaiter says.

'More than okay, thank you so much,' Áine says, and sits down.

'And I'll have a waiter clear off the other setting.'

'Actually,' Áine says. She hesitates. She had rehearsed this too for Miles. 'Could you, actually, leave it? It's just …' She looks pleadingly at the other woman, who nods slowly and smiles. Sympathy – there it is. Hated and craved for.

'That's no problem at all. Enjoy your meal.'

Áine puts down her menu and raises her glass of Gewürztraminer. Suzie would have talked about its 'notes'. She bows her head, takes a sip. The food comes and is eaten perfunctorily. There is a glass of wine with each course, which the sommelier describes to her, but she downs them all in a couple of gulps. She does not register the fermented horseradish sauce with the halibut. Suzie would have been oohing and aahing about it for weeks. The cheeses could be putty; she barely touches them. The restaurant fills. A couple sits at the adjacent table and, of course, the woman immediately notices her and pays close attention. Áine stares at the seat opposite and the place setting, willing herself not to cry or bolt for the door, diners glancing after her, put-out that their expensive evening has been encroached-upon by some emotionally wrought woman.

The George is heaving. A throb of sound and heat pushes against her when she walks past the bouncers and opens the door. What did she expect on a Saturday night? She should have set up a date on the HER App in advance. Too old for this, by far. The DJ in the corner, wearing what looks like a Madonna 1980s outfit, thumps out a tarted-up Lionel Richie song. Áine takes a deep breath. She's also eaten too much; she should have had the *à la carte*.

She puts on that look. The one like she belongs, like she's not desperate, like she might already be meeting somebody but you'd never know your luck, baby. She leans on the crowded bar and orders a vodka and Slimline Tonic from a Cillian Murphy lookalike. From that film, *Breakfast on Pluto*.

A small little thing, who appears to be about twelve, tries to get her attention from a nearby table. She might be seventeen. Áine watches her, and nods warily. On cue, the twelve-year-old, or seventeen-year-old – or whatever age she is – approaches, all smiles. She looks familiar.

'Hi, you don't remember me, do you?' she says. She's wearing a Twiggy-like, sequined mini-dress. She actually looks a bit like a young Twiggy, with that pixie crop. Pretty, but a bit on the small and skinny side. Still, beggars can't be choosers.

'You look very familiar,' Áine says.

'I'm Claudia Goggin, you taught me Irish in Richmond Hill.'

'Oh Jesus. A good few years ago, I hope.'

'Long enough,' Claudia says. 'Em, are you meeting someone? Would you like to join us? Or me, I should say. My friend is just leaving.'

'I'd be delighted,' Áine says. She wonders if she is really going to do this. Really? Pick up an ex-student in a bar? But why not? Claudia must be over twenty-one by now and Suzie had made it plain that they were both free agents. *Keep going you idiot*, she tells herself on the way to their table, it's what you wanted isn't it? Don't stop now – you won't break her.

Opening the hotel bedroom door, she senses a stiffness in Claudia. A distance. It began in the lift. Perhaps she's getting cold feet. Áine badly wants to kiss her again and pull that Twiggy dress off her. By now Suzie would have had her leggings and panties down around her ankles. She fights back the thought, and calms down.

'Red wine okay?' Áine says.

'Oh, sure, I'm easy. But you already know that,' Claudia says.

'I wouldn't say that. You already got about five dances out of me.'

'God, this room is lovely. I've walked past this place so many times.'

'Pity the bar was closed, it's kinda cool.'

'So, I meant to ask you. Are you around for a while?' Claudia says, with a little too much nonchalance.

'No, heading back tomorrow, after the game. School on Monday don't you know.' Áine pours two glasses of wine and gives one to Claudia, who has shed her heels and sits on the bed, her skinny legs tucked under her.

'Oh, yes, the All-Ireland. I forgot. Oh, hey! Didn't you used to play camogie for Cork?' She takes a sip of wine and leans out and puts the glass on the bedside locker.

'I did. Won two All-Irelands actually,' Áine says.

'Wow. In Croke Park?' Claudia says.

'The very place. Now, for camogie it isn't full or anything like it'll be tomorrow. But still.'

'Fantastic. How did you get into it? Camogie, I mean?'

'School, I suppose, and my father and my brother played hurling. Glen Rovers. It's a big deal on the northside.' Images of her father come to her. That first time he brought her to Thurles, for the Centenary All-Ireland final. The night she sat her parents down and broke the news, her father trying to mask his sorrow. The poor man gasping for breath only a few years later in Marymount Hospice, willing his life to be over.

'What's that like? Stepping out onto Croke Park for an All-Ireland final?'

'Pretty cool,' Áine says. The dressing room before the finals, sick with fear. Sprinting out onto that pitch with her teammates, whom she'd have died for. The relief afterwards, Jesus, the sweetness of it. Followed by the joy and the pride. Goosebumps tramp up and down her neck and arms. She feels her back straighten, her chest rise. 'Actually, it's amazing.'

'And you did it,' Claudia says.

'And I did it,' Áine says. There is something new in Claudia's eyes. Áine pays closer attention.

'Well if you did that, do you think you could come over here and kiss me? Like, now?'

Áine smiles, rises from the armchair and goes to her.

Áine has to turn the Victorian-looking showerhead all the way around to get any heat. It's still not hot enough for her. But it's powerful and she loves a shower to loosen out her muscles before an early morning run. Claudia is a late bird; she's made that clear. Didn't even turn over when Áine left the bed and wrote a hasty note. She'll look in on her before she heads out.

She closes her eyes as the shower heats up. She presses her head against the shiny blue wall tiles, letting the water scald her shoulders and her neck.

Áine strolls through a wakening Temple Bar in her red jersey. She is relieved the parting had been so easy and surprised that she asked Claudia for a date in two weeks in Cork. Hurling fans mix with tourists. Traditional Irish music is being piped out of a pub – a slow reel. A large Cork contingent drinks and chats outside The Palace Bar and she salutes two women from Newtown, whose names she can't remember.

Mulligans is packed, even though it's only 12.30, mostly with Cork people. The adults: excited, hopeful, flooring pints. The children: bored, sucking orange and coke out of bottles with straws. There is a beery smell from the place – a warm, fuggy, dimness. Lines of Guinness settle on the counter-top. She weaves her way through the buzz of conversation and laughter and says hello to Johnny Cremin from Newcestown, whose sister used to play with the Cork Junior team. She sees her brother, Kieran, and his wife, Trish, in the corner under the television. Trish's sister, Maura, is deep in conversation with some old guy with a flat cap. She draws men to her like flowers draw bees – they just can't help themselves. Áine has always been sorry that she's as straight as a die. The best ones usually are.

'Yay, Áine's here,' Trish shouts and gives her a hug.

'Well, the dead arose and appeared to many,' Kieran says, and he looks at his watch. Áine can see a glittering in his eye. The pint of lager he's holding isn't his first.

'Hey, I was out running at eight this morning, boy.'

'You were, yeah.'

'It's true. Drink anyone?'

'Same again. Heineken,' Kieran says.

Maura extricates herself from the old man and gives Áine a longer hug than is strictly necessary. Maura is a worrier. And clued in.

'How's my favourite lezzer?' she says, gaily.

'Not bad, Maura. Got my hole last night, so I'm happy out.'

'Jesus!' Kieran says. 'You can't say that!'

'Why not, if it's true?' Áine says.

'Because I can't be fucking hearing it,' he says. 'Now I have that in my head for the day. I'm going to the jacks.' He slouches off.

'Don't mind him, the big baby,' Trish says. 'Tell us all about it. Was she a lasher?'

'She's an old student of mine,' Áine says.

'You're kidding!' Maura says. Her eyes sparkle with mischief.

'I'll tell you all about it when I get a drink, I'm gasping,' Áine says, feeling at home.

The light on Butt Bridge is blinding after the darkness of the pub. Halfway across, Áine turns to the river and shouts: 'Up the Rebels!' She wants not to be nervous, she wants the three pints to have calmed her down.

Gardiner Street Lower is full of light and colour. The crowds thicken as they make their way up the hill and into Mountjoy Square.

'Maura, if I could meet somebody like you, I'd be laughing. I'd be set up for life,' Áine says. She has her arm around Maura's shoulder.

'You will too, sure,' Maura says. 'Give it a small bit of time.'

'Oh, time is running out, girl. Tick tock, tick tock.'

'Anyway, I'm taken, remember?' Maura says, showing her wedding ring.

'How *is* Gary?' Áine says, after a pause. She never knows whether to ask or not. Maura is normally the one to bring up his chronic depression whenever she wants to talk about it. But Áine can't not enquire, either.

'Oh, you know. Up and down. Actually I must try him again, his phone doesn't seem to be working.' She takes out her phone, presses the screen and holds it to her ear. After a few seconds she sighs, presses the screen again and puts it back in her bag.

'No joy?' Áine says. Maura shakes her head.

'How are Jenny and Cass?'

'They're fine, altogether. Look,' Maura says, and shows her the phone screensaver. Two beautiful girls, the image of their mother, grinning in T-shirts and shorts on a beach.

'Awww, that's lovely, Maura,' Áine says. 'God, Jenny is getting tall.'

'She is.' Maura smiles. 'They're all hyped up about the match. Wanted to come with me.'

'Next year, maybe.'

'Yeah. Next year,' Maura says. She looks down. 'Anyway, let's win this today first.'

'Yeah,' says Kieran. 'Oh to, oh to be, oh to be a rebel!'

They all sing lustily. Others around join in.

As they make their way down Fitzgibbon Street, her first sight of Croke Park is a punch in the stomach. A hollowed-out, tight feeling stays with her all the way down Jones' Road. The others leave her at the barrier to go to the Cusack Stand. She is in the Lower Hogan.

Inside the ground, she drinks some water and tries to calm herself. She says hello to old camogie comrades and their families. She eats a sandwich with a cup of tea and it stays down. Everything is a bit blurry, too bright and too loud – as if she were hungover. She buys a Heineken and stands near the bar and reads the programme. Larry and Stephen Murphy from Mallow, who are drinking pints of Guinness from plastic glasses, recognise her and start up a conversation. One of them nods to her as a nervous-looking middle-aged couple walk by.

'See them?' he says. 'That's Sean Culloty's mam and dad. Michael and Anne.'

She takes them in. The man is low-sized but fit-looking in a sports coat and grey pants with an incongruous pair of walking shoes. The woman, who has short hair and glasses, wears a light summer dress, with a red cardigan around her shoulders. Her face is flushed.

Áine tries to imagine how they are feeling. When she goes to her seat, she notices that the Cullotys are three rows behind her. She wonders if it wouldn't be better to watch the match on TV, in the hotel across the road. She tries to take it all in, to be present.

A few minutes into the second half, she realises that she can't follow the ball. The noise is too loud. The sun is too bright. She's hemmed in all around. What's the fucking point of it all? Her knees hop up and down. As if they do not belong to her, as if they are on somebody else's body. She looks at them, willing them to stop. She shoves her elbows down against them.

She presses her face into her hands and runs her fingers through her hair. The man beside her indicates something to his wife. The couple switch seats.

'Are you okay?' the woman says. 'What's wrong, love? We're still in it.'

Áine tries to speak but words won't come. She nods instead. She doesn't want to look at the woman. Clare score another point and there is a groan from the Cork supporters around her. She does that stupid thing, waving at her own face, as if that will stop her tears. She swallows.

'I'm okay. I'm okay,' she says, breathlessly. But the woman knows better.

'Do you have anybody around belonging to you, love?' she asks.

'No, I'm fine. Honestly,' Áine says and makes the mistake of looking at her.

She is maybe mid-fifties and her face is lined as though she has been years out in the sun. A smoker. The strained look of a mother. She puts a hand on Áine's shoulder. Áine grabs her jacket and bag.

She sidles out, stumbling past the row of supporters. Some of them grumble as she blocks their view. Clare win another free. She runs up steps and down steps onto the open area outside. A young man with a high-viz jacket sweeps papers and empty plastic glasses along the ground. She rushes past, towards the exit. The main exit gate is still closed and she realises with horror that she might not be able to get out. The turnstiles are closed too. She runs up to two men with peaked caps and walkie-talkies.

'I have to get out. I have to get out,' she says. They look at her with alarm.

'Go over there, love. Go down them steps, right? There's a gate there and they'll let yez out,' the older man says. She runs to the gate and a fat man quickly opens it and stands aside.

The metal clangs behind her. She forms her lips into an 'O', willing her heart to slow down. She leans her head back and exhales deeply, savouring the surge of freedom, of escape. The panic has been replaced by a sore emptiness, what you feel after a long bout of retching. She wipes her eyes and turns towards the railway bridge. A cheer spews from the ground. The street is almost empty. A flag seller, smoking a rollie, scrolls on his phone. A huckster stocks up on bottles of soft drinks.

Áine buys a bottle of water and drinks from it greedily. She turns right before the bridge behind Hill 16. It looks like a dead-end and she is about to turn back when she sees the little opening of a tunnel. She continues on underneath it. Two guards, standing at the entrance, watch her closely. She walks under the railway line and down the narrow path between the backs of houses and lock-ups on one side and a high wall almost covered with briars and small trees on the other. There is a groan followed by a hush from inside the ground. An explosion of sound and the Cork fans on The Hill chant: 'Rebels! Rebels! Rebels! Rebels!' over and over and over. She drinks more water and staggers on.

At the end of the path, two boys in tracksuits with gelled hair and hopeful moustaches lean against a van.

'Any cigarettes, missus? Got a Euro for a sandwich?'

She ignores them, looking for something to give her bearings. The road she's on brings her back into the stadium, and not towards the city. She turns around and stumbles and begins to cry.

A sustained tumultuous roar erupts from behind her and she quickens her pace. Two nearby guards look at a phone and one shakes his head and says: 'Those Cork fuckers.'

At a junction there is a shop with the sign 'Daybreak Store Clonliffe Road' and she knows where she is. Her phone gives several beeps. Text and Facebook messages. The last is a text from Claudia.

Enjoy the celebrations!

She looks at another one, from Sinead Moriarty, her friend in Boston.

Looking good now, Culloty is some man. Sully's on fire.

She stops walking and opens her Twitter feed.

@GAAOfficial #AllIrelandHurling Cork 2–14 Clare 1–13. FT #nowherelikeit #rebelsabu

She laughs into her hand, through the tears. She leans against a car. She turns right onto Ballybough Road. An ambulance, siren blaring, screams past her. Her phone beeps and beeps and then rings. She looks at the number. It is a 001 number not in her contacts.

'Hello,' she says warily.

'Hello, Áine. It's Suzie.'

Her feet stop.

'Áine? Áine? Can you hear me?'

'Hello,' she manages.

'I just wanted to say congratulations. I was listening on the radio. Are you delighted?'

Huge cheers in the distance. Another ambulance screams past.

'Áine? Can you hear me? Is the line bad? That sounds like an ambulance. Is everything okay?'

'Everything's fine. Just an ambulance going past. You know Dublin.'

'How are you? Are you thrilled?'

Áine moves the phone away from her ear and looks at the screen. Suzie says something she cannot hear. Áine holds her thumb over the round red symbol with the white phone in its centre. She presses it.

Áine is on Summerhill going past more flats. She wonders why she has a stitch in her side. The phone rings again. The same US number. She presses 'Reject'. She switches off the phone. She holds onto a high green railing. There are crows in the waste ground behind it. Clare fans walk past. A teenage girl glares at her. Miraculously, she sees an empty taxi on Gardiner Street. She waves and it stops. She almost falls into it.

'Clarence Hotel,' she says. She leans back into the headrest and closes her eyes.

She puts a brave face on it in the hotel lobby. Luka is away collecting another car so she will have a long wait. Baptiste notices her strain.

'Did you win the match?' he says. *Ze match.*

'Yes, yes we did, actually, Baptiste. Up the Rebels.'

'Always, up the rebels, Áine,' he says, smiling. He is a very handsome man. Áine sits in one of the large soft armchairs and manages not to turn on her phone for ten minutes. Until she can manage no longer.

Two missed calls from the US number. A new voicemail message. She almost activates it. She scrolls down through the texts, her Facebook and Twitter feeds. Her friend Gillian Power has posted a selfie on Instagram with Sean Culloty, however the hell she got to him. The message reads: 'two legends'. Trust Gillian.

Another text comes through. Maura.

Galtee Inn in Cahir for steaks? (hope it went ok)

Suddenly there is only home, the need to be home. Hurry up, Luka. She puts away the phone. The battery's at eight per cent.

A heavy-set Corkman comes through the hotel door with a beautiful young boy in a Cork jersey.

'Cheer up, girl,' the man says, passing towards the bar. 'We won!'

She smiles up at him. 'We did, indeed,' she says. She smiles at the boy. 'Up the Rebels!' she says.

He grins back and punches the air with two little fists. 'Yesss,' he says.

The traffic out of the city is brutal, but at least her phone is charging. On the Naas Road, she presses the Voicemail button and holds her breath.

'Hi, Áine, I keep getting cut off. Maybe reception is bad there, or maybe you don't want to talk to me. Look, I just wanted to call to say congratulations. I know how much it means to you. I wish

I could be there with you. I really do. I,' Suzie pauses and sighs. 'This is my new number. Ring me back if you can. I'd love to talk. I'll be travelling a lot, in China mostly. So … you have my email too, the gmail one is best. Bye, Áine. Bye.'

Áine replays the message and sniffles and looks for a tissue in her bag but there are none left. She leaves out a wail that frightens her. She almost drives into the car in front, which has slowed. She blows her horn relentlessly at it.

Her phone beeps again, another text message. At the next stoppage, she checks it.

Well? Cahir for shteak and shpuds?

She smiles and sniffles and taps on the screen.

C U there. Mine's a big fat fillet.

A reply comes back immediately.

You're a big fat fillet.

Áine laughs.

Angels

Is this really happening?

Are you here, sitting in front of the TV, right now, this minute, waiting for the match to start, drinking can after can of beer? Or is it somebody else, not you?

Did you do that? You couldn't have.

Do what?

Did you take a pillow to Jenny and Cass upstairs, after drugging them? Like you'd planned for weeks. Was that you?

Ah, but it was. You did. Or did you? You're not sure. How can you not be sure of something like that?

The girls are in their beds upstairs. You're almost certain of it. You look around the room – well, they're not here, where else could they be? You crushed up the Halcion tablets first thing this morning, with the mortar and pestle, when Maura left to go to the match. You cried as you were doing it, the sound of the tablets cracking like dried bones. Then you sprinkled the powder into their hot chocolate. You did.

You did.

You try to remember if you put the pillow over their precious sleeping faces, or if you just stood there with it trembling in your hands, walking back and forth at the end of the beds, talking to yourself. The clear morning sunlight flowed through the window, reflecting off the creamy pillowcase in your hand. You remember that powdery smell in their room. Their little chests rising and falling as they slept. Jenny's left leg bent funnily under her. Cass's *Star Wars* 'tattoo' of that robot on her forearm. Her strawberry blonde hair spilling down over her face. Those pink *Frozen* pyjamas that she insists upon wearing, night after night – with the Disneyfied, doe-eyed, heart-shaped faces of those sisters, Anna and Emma. Or is it Elsa?

Did you right Cass's hair and straighten Jenny's leg before you took the pillow to them? You can't remember. You must have.

You do know that Jenny walked groggily up the stairs and you did carry Cass up to the bed after the hot chocolate. That is definite. They are in their beds. That's for sure.

The pencil feels heavy in your fingers as you try to write some words in the notebook. But no words will come. What words are there, anyway? And what good would they do her?

You open another can, looking blankly at the screen. The sound is turned down because of the headache. You couldn't be listening to those muppets, anyway. The minor match is nearly finished. Kilkenny again, the bastards. Your phone (on Airplane Mode) says 13:57. An hour and a half to go.

She was full of it this morning, of course. Heading off to the match with Trish and that dopey husband of hers. Poured, as she'd say herself, into those white skinny jeans she thinks she's only divine in. What was that expression she had the other day about something she didn't like? Oh, yes. *I wouldn't be wild about that.* Yes. Very good when you think of it, but the opposite doesn't work. *I'm wild about that.* No. You can say, *I'm crazy about that*, all right. Can you say *I'm not crazy about that?*

Speaking of crazy, take another Tofranil there, while you think of it, boy. Take two, to be sure to be sure.

You open another can. These slabs of beer are great value, only €20 for twenty-four cans. You hear a song from the radio in the kitchen: 'Breakfast in America'. E.L.O. Or is it Supertramp? You sing along about the girls in California, a vision entering your mind of blue skies and blonde young women in bikinis on a beach.

You 'na na na' yourself off into reverie and then you sleep. You dream about walking down a never-ending hospital corridor. It's in John of Gods, of course, and yet it isn't. In the way that dreams have of bringing you somewhere that isn't really there. It is John of Gods because you know it is. It isn't because there are no zombie patients shuffling around in tracksuit pants and stained T-shirts; no kind-faced nurses or competent-faced psychiatrists; no bloat-faced, doped-up, stubbled ex-architects looking out at you from mirrors. No smells or mumbling or shame or terror.

You wake up. Can you even smell in dreams? It bothers you. You try to recall if you ever have. There are ads on the TV and you have a sudden horror that you slept out. 14:29. Phew. An hour to go. A bit of a lurch when you get up, but you right yourself. Have to tidy the place up. You pick up some empty cans and the hot chocolate cups – one *Star Wars*, one *Frozen*. You smell the dregs in the cups. Nothing. No wonder they use it to drug girls and rape them. Another thing you're saving them from.

Altruistic filicide – you count them, seven syllables. Sounds almost innocuous. Stupid name, Halcion, too, when you think of it. Should be called Somnium, or something like that.

The sunlight in the kitchen assaults your eyes and takes you back to the incessant rows when you were redesigning the house. When you'd show her the new drawings.

'I thought we were going to have the island *here*,' she said, pointing to the centre of the room on the plan.

'Yeah, it kind of blocks the flow there. If we have it here, we'll get the benefit of the French doors and the view outside.'

'Fuck the fucking flow of the room, I wanted it there. It's the one thing I asked you, the one thing – to have my own kitchen. But no. The flow of the room. Jesus Christ,' she said, storming out and slamming the door behind her.

She never got her island in the end. Events intervened, didn't they? Events, dear boy. But you were right, too, it would have blocked the flow. Not that it matters now. The bank will probably take the house anyway, along with everything else.

You put the cups in the dishwasher. Must turn that on, too.

It all seems so unreal. Or surreal. Maybe you're dreaming the whole thing. Maybe you'll wake up in a minute and it'll be …

Be what?

Be fine?

Be over?

She'll have 'lover boy' to console her, of course. The barefaced cheek of her, denying it to your face when you eventually built up the courage to confront her. It was all in your head, she had no interest whatsoever in any other man, you invented the whole thing. She thinks you're some fool, laughing at you behind your back, but we'll see who has the last laugh. She can go and fuck him all she wants now. See how she enjoys it now. She can make two more kids for herself with him and see how that works out. But she's not getting yours. Oh, no, they're yours. They stay with you.

Anyway, the literature was quite clear: Resnick's study catalogued the motives for filicide as: 1) altruistic (*tick*); 2) acutely psychotic (*tick, probably*); 3) accidental filicide (e.g. maltreatment) (*no tick*); 4) unwanted child (*no tick*); and 5) spouse revenge (*tick*).

Three out of five. And when you add in the history of depression (*tick*), previous self-harm (*tick*), mental illness (*tick*), consumption of alcohol and medication (*tick tick*), and fear of spousal estrangement (*tick tick tick*), that's a lot of ticking. Which reminds you.

You look at the kitchen clock. 3:14, getting close now. They'll be on the pitch already. If they can only mark McMahon, they'll do it. *Sully's scoring goals, he's scoring goals.*

If you're psychotic, can you be aware that you're psychotic? Wouldn't that negate the psychosis, if it's true? Just because you're paranoid doesn't mean they're not out to get you.

You check yourself – you wonder sometimes if you're saying out loud what you're thinking. No. It's quiet.

Another thing: isn't it fair to say that if life is hard (*which it is*) and full of pain and suffering (*which it is*) and then you fall in love and get dumped (*which you do*) and then you're alone and lonely (*which you are*) and then you get depressed (*which you do*) and then you can't work (*which you can't*) and then you are poor (*which you will become*) and then you are stressed to the gills (*which you are*) and then you get old (*which you do*) and then you get sick (*which you will*) and then you die in misery (*inevitably*), isn't it better to prevent all that?

Isn't it?

To have never suffered pain or worry or despair? To fall asleep painlessly as a child and never to wake up? As an innocent? Pure and clean? To become angelic, to become, in fact, an angel. Angels – that's what they looked like in their two beds and that's what they will always be now. Perfect. Washed pure in the sunlight. Buried side by side in their little white coffins in their good dresses. Beautiful and pure. Daddy's little angels.

And you there with them. Beside them in the ground. Looking after them, forever.

Will that happen? Will it, though?

You bend over. You moan. You hold on to the sink for support. You press your forehead against the sun-warmed white ceramic.

You wander back into the living room. Stagger, really. You flop on the sofa. Need to keep on top of things, but fuck it. You open another can from the slab. You think about turning up the sound, but no, this is better. Both teams are parading behind the band. The players form two lines for the national anthem and face the flag. After that, they take their places around the pitch. Here we go. Clare bastards. Up the Rebels!

Looks like they put Culloty on McMahon at left half-back. Good move. The game begins. You sip your beer and settle down to fret.

The game is shit. Cork are hanging on for dear life. Sully hardly touches the ball. Lucky to be just a couple of points down at half-time.

You take a well-earned piss in the downstairs toilet. Coming back into the living room, you stand and stare for several moments at the carpeted stairs through the door. No going back upstairs, not now. Angels. Daddy's angels, forever.

You wake up on the sofa. Did you fall asleep again? Shit, you did. How could you have fallen asleep at a time like this? You look at the TV but can't focus. You're groggy; must be all the beer.

You look for the packet with the fifteen metres of rope on the coffee table; it isn't there. It was earlier, you're almost certain. You bought it six months ago, surprised that the shortest rope you could get was fifteen metres long.

Did you bring it in from the shed earlier and put it on the table? Did you open the packet and make the noose like you learned on YouTube and wrap it around two of the banisters? You're almost certain you did. Or did you imagine it?

The match is over and the muppets are talking in silence. They start laughing, whatever's funny. It switches to show Sean Culloty accept the cup and raise it above his head. Did Cork win?

You look to your left.

Two little pale waifs are standing by the door in their little bare feet. Two angels. Cass in her *Frozen* pyjamas, Eeyore hanging from her right hand. Jenny in her long nightdress, the back of her index finger in her mouth, the way she does when she's anxious; her hair over her eye, the way it hangs there.

Your angels.

Jenny has grown so tall. She's the image of your sister, Eva, at that age – all gangly arms and legs. She's looking straight at you, her head swaying slightly.

Cass is staring at the TV. Her eyes are wide, replete with wonder, and she gives a shiver of excitement. She says something; you almost don't hear her. She says, 'Oh.'

You feel your face fall in upon itself. It fissures and caves in and something escapes out of it. Some untenable sound.

Is this really happening?

Her Mother Evelyn

The birthdays are the worst. I tend to walk through them in a daze. Mind you, Roisín, it's a daze for which I'm glad – and not the type of daze I suffered from when I was taking all that medication. I hated the foggy feeling that stuff used to give me. For your birthdays, on the fifteenth of May – although of course it's not just your birthday, is it? – I spend a lot of time in the back garden, even if it's raining. There's always something to do that time of year, thank God. The weeds are flying up, and the first chrysanths are out, and the delphiniums and the irises near the hedge, and the lilies and the poppies – it's all go. I bring the small radio with me to distract myself. I couldn't go out in case I'd meet somebody. Tim tends to rise early and go straight in to work and come home late after one of his meetings. It's better if we're not around each other on those days; we'd probably tear strips off each other. Or I'd tear strips off him – he was never any good at fighting with me. He never was any good at hating; even in his hurling heyday when he'd knock the block off some lad from Tipp or Kilkenny, it was never personal. But I can hate. Oh yes, I can hate very well indeed.

The only person your father ever hated was himself, and he's still good at that – though not as good as when he was drinking. I think it's mainly because he never fought back against my father over Sean. He was only eighteen and my father was a piece of work, but of course Tim blames himself.

You'd be twenty now, if you'd lived. Sean – who I still think of as James, the name we gave him, the name he'd still have if he'd stayed ours – he'll be twenty-nine before we know it.

Twenty-nine years.

So that's forty-eight birthdays between the two of ye and another in a few months. That's a lot of birthdays without a party.

When I think about it now, I have gone through three main phases of reaction to the question: *And do you have children yourself, Evelyn?* My first, when I was younger and frail (I was sick for a long time after you died, love), was to redden and fluster and blurt out a *no* – which embarrassed the life out of the questioner because it wasn't just a *no, not yet*, or a *no, I've no interest*, it was (and I'm sure this was very obvious, too), it was a *no, no I don't and it's all I want in the world and now it's never going to happen* kind of a *no*.

Later on, when I had no hope of a reunion with Sean (and I was angry about that for a long time), and when, if I'm honest (and I'm a bit ashamed of this), I had gone into a kind of denial about you too – about ever having had you at all; then I used to give a cold *no*, a curt *no*, a this is the end of the conversation, what a rude question, what kind of person are you even to ask it, kind of a *no*. And the person (it's nearly always a woman, though Tim probably gets it from men), sure she just wanted to chat and talk about her own children. There'd be a terrible silence after I spoke, a frightful thing altogether that froze the air around me, and even seemed to block out the light, and all I'd want to do is run away and hide.

And now? Now I give a smiling *no*, or a matter of fact, almost casual *no*, or a *no* maybe with a hint of regret. But it's a measured kind of regret, poles apart from the raging guilt that almost consumed me when I had to be admitted to St Pat's – a place I thought at one time I'd never be leaving. I always say back: *And what about yourself?* So then she has permission to talk about her own children and I can pretend to be interested, and ask some of the usual types of questions back. Or maybe she had already been talking about her children, in which case I'll say something like: *And what age are yours now?* or *So is it only the two you have?* Something like that. It's mostly when I'm golfing with people who don't know me that the question arises these days, and I'm always on guard, ready for it.

I don't think golf would really be you, Roisín. Definitely not, at twenty – that would be all wrong.

Now I'm going to let you in on a little secret. I gave another answer too, for a while. Not often, but I did it and I'm a bit ashamed – I never told anyone about it. Sometimes I used to say *yes*. When somebody asked me if I had children, I used to say, *yes, I've two, James and Roisín* and I'd give whatever ages you were at the time. I'd say that James was in college and you were in such-and-such a year in secondary school, or that he was in secondary and you were in primary, and I used to say that you were a handful (sorry about that, love) and that James was quiet and studious and a hurler like his father. But I'd feel terrible afterwards and I'd be afraid that the person might say something to somebody who knew me, and people would talk about me and think I was queer in the head. So I stopped doing that. I haven't said *yes* to the question for years, now, and I don't think I'll ever do it again.

Tim tried to hide his nerves this morning before he headed off to the match with Pat. Neither of us slept, of course, but that's nothing new. I don't know how he can stand watching Sean on the pitch at all. It's a terrible rough game. I couldn't bear to watch your father play, either, even when we were going out first. I suppose losing a final must be hard, too. But Tim seems to think Cork will win and that gave me a little prick of hope.

I tell myself it's never going to happen and I should just keep seeing out the days, one by one, as best I can. But Tim might mention him, or I'd hear a story about a late reunion on the radio or the television (there was a series about adoption on TV3 last year), or I'd go on the Internet and I'd think: *Why not?* He's only twenty-eight and I'm only forty-six. There's plenty of time.

So lately I've had this silly idea that if Cork do win, that Sean might change his mind, that something might be triggered in him that will make him want to make contact – with his father, especially. And I know, I know, I'm probably grasping at straws and I'm setting myself up for another fall and I feel so foolish whenever the phone rings and I think *that might be the social worker now,* or when I hear Liam's van at the bottom of the drive.

I used to stand by the window in the front room and watch out for Liam – he always delivers just after eleven. I did it for a long time. I'd imagine all sorts of things while I was standing there, looking out through the blinds. All sorts of things, Roisín. About where we'd meet him, and how it would be, and how he'd get on with his father, and how they could talk about hurling and I could ask him about his job, or Michael and Anne, or his girlfriend. My excitement, on the days when Liam would pull up and put something in the box. I'd count to a hundred and go out the back door and slowly walk down the drive, as if I was just going down to pick up the post, maybe say hello to Mick next door, on the way. Just walking down to the gate.

Whereas in reality my heart would be pounding and I'd be praying 'Hail Holy Queen' all the way down. *Hail Holy Queen, Mother of Mercy, hail our life, our sweetness and our hope.*

And my hand shaking as I open the flap, hoping upon hope to see the Tusla stamp on a letter or some other indication that it's Sean wanting to make contact with us, wanting us to be part of his life.

But it's never there, Roisín. It never is. It probably never will be.

Then I'd have to turn around and walk back to the house with a bill or some brochure in my hand. Maybe chat to Mick or Helen on the way, and do a bit of cleaning around the house, or listen to the radio, or make myself a cup of tea and pretend that everything is fine.

The dahlias look nice in the vase, don't they? The pink ones are lovely altogether. It was a great idea of Tim's to dig a little hole on the grave so that the vase goes into it and can't fall over. It almost seems like the dahlias are growing there above you, along with the petunias. I suppose I could plant some too. Anyway, I'll put in fresh water tomorrow and take a little off the stems – there's no sign of rain. That fold-up secateurs is the best thing I ever bought, and I want this place to be nice for you, pet. I do want that. For me too, being selfish.

I feel bad sometimes that I never told your father about the time I made contact with Michael and Anne all those years ago. I feel terrible guilty about it. He's been sober for so long now that I think I could, but he'd be very hurt. If Sean ever does make contact, and he won't now – if he was going to do it, he would have done it when he turned eighteen – but if he does, sure I can tell him then. He'll be so happy it won't matter. It was a kind of betrayal, I know that, but he was in and out of recovery at the time and I didn't want to risk a relapse. At least I did something to get Sean back, seeing as how Tim did nothing. Not one single thing.

But if he knew that I told Sean who *he* was, that his father was the great Tim Collins; if he knew that Sean had known all along and never said anything, never approached him. I dread to think what would happen. So I keep saying nothing. I'm good at it.

Or maybe it's my way of getting back at him, my revenge for his years of drunkenness and for our chance at adoption that we missed out on because he wouldn't countenance it. Whenever I tried to talk to him about it, he'd storm off to get drunk somewhere and I mightn't see him for days. Oh, I was fierce angry with him over all the drinking and him being missing all the time, and me at home on my own like a fool waiting for him, and all the awful things he'd say when he'd stagger in the door. I still am angry. I am, but I don't want to think about it any more, what's the point of dwelling on it? I don't know if that's the reason I never told him, but it could be. Like I say, I'm good at being angry and I'm very good at hiding it. When I go over to my mother and father's graves after I leave you I'll bottle it up tight and say a prayer for them as if I mean it.

And it *was* wrong too – what I told them, about the hereditary health issues and everything. It was blackmail, really. Poor Anne, the day I said that to her in the Vienna Woods. But I wasn't in my right mind, I wasn't, and he was *my* son, too. I don't like to think about that any more, either.

When I met Sean that day in the hotel – you should have seen him, Roisín – when he walked through the door. Oh, sweet Jesus. He was perfect, he was only perfect, so tall with dark hair and brown eyes like all the Collinses, and he was frightened, trying to be brave, the poor thing, the fear in his eyes. He was only fifteen, just turned fifteen, it was December, a week after his birthday and I was going to bring him a present but the social worker wouldn't allow me. All I wanted to do was to hold him, just to put my arms around him – if only I could have held him – but the social worker also warned me not to be tactile, so I didn't. I'm sorry now. Tactile – what a horrible, stupid word. I wasn't supposed to tell him who his father was, either. No identifying information, she warned me, but that just slipped out, I just blurted it out and he was entitled to know, anyway, he had every right.

And when I walked into the hotel that day, you know what I thought, Roisín? I thought it would be the end of my misery and that I'd have him back, at least in some form. I was sure of it. I knew he wouldn't be walking out the door with me instead of Anne – I mean, I wasn't that stupid to think we'd live happily ever after and I'd bring him home to Tim and take care of him forever the way that I was always meant to. Things don't work like that.

But when I never heard back from him again, not a word, even after he turned eighteen – and I never found out why, I never found out, and I still don't know why. Well, I tried to console myself: at least I'd had that meeting. At least he saw me and I saw him and

I talked to him, and he knows me, he knows who I am and he knows that I exist and that I love him and that I never wanted to give him up, that my father made me and Tim was too young to fight the bully. At least he knows that, even if he never did make contact again and probably never will. At least I have that.

I suppose it's some consolation.

I had a lovely morning today, really, despite all the nerves. After Tim left, I sat in the conservatory in my dressing gown and drank a nice cup of tea in the sun, and I listened to that beautiful music on Lyric, and thought about you and Sean. I went to nine o'clock Mass and it was Father O'Reilly and he gave a nice sermon about forgiveness, which was a kind of comfort to me because I've never forgiven God for what he did to me and I never will. How could I?

After Mass I drove up to the golf club to wish Jim well on the day of his President's Prize. And Peggy too. I think the golf club saved me, in a way. It sounds stupid, I know. I didn't want to go at first and Kitty used to have to drag me there, God bless her. But I'm so glad I stuck with it. You know, every time I hit that ball on the first tee, and I put my driver back into my bag, and I'm standing there beside one of my many friends looking down the fairway, I feel like I'm a different person. I do. That today is a new day and that this is a new round of golf and every hole is a new hole, the last one doesn't matter. The newness of it all lifts my spirits somehow, I can't explain it. But – and this might sound selfish – even if you were alive, and even if Tim ever did take it up (which he won't), I wouldn't want ye there; I'd still want it to be my thing.

Even today, when I wasn't playing, the buzz around the place and everyone in good humour and the feeling of belonging, and chatting to people, and the sunlight pouring in through the clubhouse windows and all the shining prizes and that beautiful piece of glass that Jim bought in Waterford – it was nearly all too much. I had a lovely cup of coffee and a scone with Peggy, and she was so relieved about the weather and Jim's decision to play Stableford and not Stroke, and they've had such a hard time of it, too, with his prostate, I couldn't be happier for them. I really couldn't.

Afterwards, I picked the flowers for you and had the bit of ham and brown bread and potato salad for lunch – Tim will finish that when he gets home. I had to be here during the match in case I'd be tempted to turn on the television or the radio. No, I knew, I just knew I couldn't be around the house while the match was on – I'd be in bits, imagining all sorts.

But here, here by your grave – the same grave that Tim and I will share with you someday – time stands still. I do get looks with my golfing fold-up seat. God, if anyone saw me they'd think I'm cracked, sitting here hour after hour, like that madwoman in the book by Charles Dickens, covered in dust, waiting for years in her wedding dress for her husband to come. That gave me the creeps when I read it in school. As though I was waiting for you to come back from the dead, to come out of the ground like from another birth, but healthy this time, and that I had to be here to pick my little baby up from the grass and not leave you lying in the cold.

The times I'd wake Tim in the middle of the night and tell him that we had to go to the grave, that you weren't dead, you weren't, it was all a big mistake and that if we went to the grave, you'd be there, lying there, just waiting for us, but healthy. I'd be raving at him and he'd have to try to calm me down or get me to take another tablet, or even phone Mary Hannon, my psychiatrist, for help. Which I did a few times, God love her, and the saint of a woman that she is, she took the calls too.

I thought about bringing a book, but that wouldn't be right, somehow. I prefer just to chat, anyway. But the looks did bother me so here's what I do now. Whenever I hear a car pull up outside, I get up off my little seat and walk around – people never stay for long and when the graveyard is busy I brazen them out, and then I do sit down again and say the odd prayer, or just breathe like Mary taught me in the hospital, all those years ago. That wonderful woman who saved my life and whom I give thanks for every blessed day.

She had no time for closure, either, and I always admired her for that. That's an over-rated word. As if being closed somewhere, boxed up and ready for delivery was a good thing. When I think of that word, I think of the moment they closed the little white coffin on you – it was so tiny, Roisín, and you were so small and they still closed you up in it, though I begged them not to. As if being closed is better than being open, or having no hope was better than having some – even if it's a false hope, who knows? Who knows, anyway? I can't hope for you any more but I know you don't mind if I still hope for Sean.

Tim said that Sean was going out with a girl from Glanmire – childhood sweethearts, he heard. *Like us?* I nearly asked him, but I didn't because that wouldn't be a good comparison and I wouldn't wish that on anybody. If they get married, and I know you don't have to get married to have children – if anyone knows, it should be me – but imagine holding another baby, my very own grandchild, to mind and to feed and to fuss over. You know, nobody will ever call me Mam or Mammy – they just won't, how could they, even Sean won't if we're ever reunited; he'll call me Evelyn, which is fine – but if Sean and his girlfriend (I wish I knew her name), if they had a baby, then maybe that baby, some day, might call me 'Granny Evelyn'.

Imagine that, Roisín, wouldn't that be something? Of course, a baby would make you an aunt, too, and you'd have been a great aunt, I just know it, and a great role model for any girl growing up. You would too. You know, for some reason I don't see you as the marrying kind, and you're dead bloody right.

He got the hurling from his father's side, no doubt about that. He's the spitting image of your Uncle Johnny. I don't see you as a camogie player. I'm thinking something to do with art, maybe, like Gretta's son who works with that company, in – what's it called again? Graphic design. Something with computers, anyway, but not programming them, designing things on them. Or maybe an artist, a painter or sculptor – something in the arts, I think for sure – I was great at drawing, you know, I won prizes. You wouldn't be in science or business, anyway. They say that art teacher in Scoil Mhuire is fantastic; she has two or three going to art college every year – you might have been one of them.

I think you'd be a bit rebellious, a bit different from the norm, and I'd be okay with that, too, but maybe not your father so much – he's a bit old-fashioned. When I think of all the possibilities that would have been open to you, Roisín, the things that young people can do these days, girls especially, the chances we didn't have in our time, oh, my heart breaks.

And who can blame me if I do talk to you? Who can judge me for that, even if it's silly oul talk, and probably not good for me, can't I even have that of you, when I've lost everything else? Would anybody begrudge me that? Ah, they wouldn't, and if they do, well feck them anyway.

When Sean decides to make contact, I think he'll phone Tim. Sure the company is in the phone book. I can picture Tim coming straight home to tell me. He wouldn't do it over the phone. I picture myself looking out the front window thinking, *God, Tim is home early, I wonder has he news?* And he'll come in through the front door and not the back door and he'll just stand there and look at me, with tears in his eyes; he'll hardly be able to speak, and he'll come to me and hold me and tell me. I can see it all so clearly.

It's nearly half-past five; he'd surely have rung by now if they won. Oh, God, maybe I should have gone to the church instead of here. But I love it here, too, and I think this is where I was meant to be. It's so peaceful and calming somehow, especially early in the morning and late in the evening, when the birds are singing.

Someday – who knows when, nobody ever knows – I'll be put in there beside you, pet. Forever. And my name will be written on that headstone, under yours.

Her mother Evelyn.

Losing

The smell of sweat and embrocation filled the air, the sound of splashing water. Big men moved quietly, to and from the showers, heads downcast. Steam oozed in along the ceiling through the open partition. The treatment table in the middle of the dressing room was heaped with towels, hurleys, bags of sliotars, helmets, a sack of training kit, two medical bags, piles of oranges and bananas, a mound of spare jerseys, five bottle-carriers of water and energy drinks, a box of energy gels, an unopened plastic packet of programmes, a crumpled large white coat.

Cillian McMahon thought he heard a sob from the corner; he did not look for the source. McGrath, the coach, and Considine, the County Board chairman, argued near the door. That prick, Considine, who had tried to get him suspended over the car crash in Lahinch. Who's great pals with his own prick of a father, of course.

McMahon looked around at the debris of his team. Quinn, the toughest full-back in Ireland, sat beside him, elbows on knees. Keane and O'Connell stared into nothingness, their jerseys off. *Lost us the game, those muppets.* James Clancy unwrapped endless bandages from around his knee and muttered to himself. Most of the others were shedding their gear. The singing and whooping of the Cork players in the distance could be heard whenever the door was opened.

Doctor Jim, crouched on one knee, stitched a gash over Shane O'Connor's eye.

'Keep still, Shane, just two to go,' he said.

'Fuck!' Quinn shouted, coming back to life. He stood up, and peeled off the inside-out Cork jersey.

McMahon opened his laces. The boot on his right foot wouldn't come off. He had to hold his shin and tug the boot free. He gasped with the pain from his ribs. *Probably fucking cracked.*

He'd been paid €1,500 to wear those boots. They looked stupid now with their garish lime-green fronts and orange laces. The insoles were completely destroyed. How could blades have done so much damage? He shoved them into his bag, out of sight.

He fought off the raw memories: his four wides, dropping that ball in the first half when he was clean through, being moved off Culloty to corner-forward, the constant mocking of Crilly, the smug look on Sullivan's face afterwards. He shook his head violently, once, like a horse shaking off flies on a hot day.

He pulled down his right sock to the heel. He tried to pick the cloth near the toes and yank it free but it wouldn't budge. Instead, he unpeeled the top of the sock with his left hand, wincing at the last, as some skin came away with it.

The sole of the upturned foot was a mess of weeping blisters and bulging sores. The ruptured skin had yellowed and slid aside, yielding the remnants of a watery red ooze. He watched it trickle down towards his heel. The uncovered fleshy patches were a vivid, blotchy red.

He pressed his thumbs into the soft inflammations and felt nothing. He placed his foot on the matted floor and pushed it down hard. He twisted it left and right, breathing through his nose.

The left stocking peeled off more easily. One bulbous swelling covered the ball of the foot, and the skin had come free from the underside of the toes. Dried blood encrusted the nail of the big toe where a Cork player had stood on it. He checked to see if the nail was cracked. Apparently not. A purplish welt, just above the ankle, marked where he'd been hit by a hurley.

He rummaged in the side pocket of his gear bag for the long scissors. Its narrow pointed tip pierced the skin of the blisters that had not already burst. He squeezed them empty with a dull satisfaction, pushing the pale liquid out with his fingernails. It dripped down on the Cork jersey at his feet. He sprinkled medicated powder onto the lesions.

He sat back on the bench and pressed his head against the wall and closed his eyes.

I'll give it good and hard to Ruth later.

He smiled at the prospect. At least he had that to look forward to.

Opening his eyes, he noticed James Ryan, an old rival of his, glaring at him from across the dressing room.

'Glad someone thinks it's funny. One point, was it?' Ryan said.

McMahon put his hand on his hurley, stood and moved forward.

'Oh, you're going to use the hurley, are you? Fucking pussy,' Ryan said, advancing.

McMahon dropped the hurley, and pressed up to Ryan, face to face. They pushed their foreheads against each other.

'Fuck you, what did you ever do in a Clare jersey? Can't even make the team,' McMahon said.

Mick Lynch, the full-forward and captain, came between them, a giant paw on either chest.

'Back off, you two. I said back off! We win together and lose together, and that's an end to it. Sit down, Cillian. Go and have your shower, you. Show a bit of pride, for fuck's sake, ye're like Rathkeale knackers the pair of ye. Young will be here in a minute and we're not going to make a show of ourselves in front of him.'

McMahon sat down, his heart racing. He stood up again, removed his togs, sat back down and put his towel on his lap. *Clarecastle shithead, shouldn't even be on the panel.*

Dinny Young, the Cork coach, entered the room with the Cork County Board secretary and they shook hands with their counterparts. Tall, tanned and fit, with short greying hair, the man looked sombre, almost apologetic.

'Lads, I won't keep ye a minute. The last thing ye want is a speech from me. We know what it feels like to come out of the wrong side of tight matches, we've lost our share of them over the past couple of years.' He took a deep breath and extended his open hands before him.

'But we've learned a lot from those defeats: how it can make us stronger. And so can ye. Ye won the All-Ireland last year with an amazing display and ye can do that again. Don't doubt it for a minute,' he said, looking straight at McMahon.

'As far as I'm concerned, each one of you has a lot to be proud of today. I know the individual sacrifices that you have made to get Clare to this final and you deserve the utmost credit for that.

You can all hold your heads high when you leave this dressing room. I believe, and I know I speak for every Cork person when I say this, that you have done your families, your clubs and your county proud – whatever today's result. And anyone who says different hasn't a clue what they're talking about.'

Young shook hands with a few players near the door and left the room, to half-hearted applause.

Cork langer, thinks he's Barack fucking Obama.

The speech reminded McMahon of what his father had said to him under the Mackey Stand after the Under 21 final two years before, when they'd lost to Limerick. In front of some of his teammates, too.

'Ye let yereselves down there today. No fucking pride in the jersey. Beaten by that bunch? Pathetic.' He had spat out the final word, and turned away and walked out through the open gate, with *her*, his so-called mother, waddling after him. Didn't even offer a lift home, or a kind word. And him on crutches, with a suspected ankle fracture. Couldn't train for three weeks.

Fucking showed you, last year. Wasn't pathetic then, was I? Five goals and twenty points from play, 1–5 in the final!

He stood up, shuffled his feet into his flip-flops and began to count the women that he had fucked in the previous twelve months. Nadine, that Dub in the back of the car, she nearly pulled the cock off him. One. Emma, who pestered him on Snapchat, then threatened to post that picture on Facebook if he didn't answer her – the bitch. Two. Rachel, from Kilkenny, three. Megan, the hippy, four. Jade, the rich bitch, five. Sarah, from Drogheda, six. The other Sarah, mad for it, anal, the works, seven. He should look her up again next year; she could be a regular when Ruth wasn't around.

He stepped into the shower cubicle and had to put his hand on the wall when the water met the soles of his feet. That one from Wexford, eight. The two that weekend in Doolin, Caitlin and Kylie, or was it Khloe? Ten. He put his head under the flow of water. He took shallow breaths to relieve the stabbing pain in his chest.

How the fuck could you have dropped that ball? It just doesn't happen.

Then Ruth. The first time was at Joe's party in that little bedroom. How many times since? Too many to count. Eleven. Maeve, the looper at Christmas, twelve. Shouldn't have done that, really; it was bad form – she was totally out of it.

The water went cold and shouts came up from the other cubicles. Typical. He dried himself down and returned to his place on the bench. He patted his feet with his towel and sprinkled more powder on them. He dressed himself slowly in his tracksuit and hoodie, instead of the suit they were supposed to wear. *Fuck them.*

'Jim, will you look at Cillian's feet. They're in bits,' Lynch said to the doctor who was flexing and icing James Clancy's knee.

'They're fine,' McMahon said. 'Just a few blisters. They're fine, Jim.'

Murphy put down the knee and gave Clancy the ice pack. 'Leave that on for ten minutes more. If it starts to burn, take it off. Have you got Nurofen?'

Clancy nodded.

'Here, give me a look,' he said to McMahon.

McMahon sighed and lifted his two feet to the bending doctor. *What a fucking nightmare.*

'Just a few blisters.'

'That's more than just a few, Cillian,' the doctor said. 'What are you putting on it?'

'This stuff. I got it from the chemist.' He handed the doctor the tin.

'Hmm, I'll give you something on the bus. Don't pull off the loose skin. Have you clean socks?'

'I was just going to wear the trainers.'

'No, if these get infected you'll be in trouble. You might need an antibiotic too, we'll see tomorrow. Rest them as much as you can. Keep them as dry as possible.'

They departed the dressing room in dribs and drabs. Most people left him alone, as he hobbled by, with his hurleys and gear bag.

Out in the tall tunnel where the bus was parked, straggling Clare supporters – mostly players' friends and relations – stood still, in clusters, bereft.

One little girl, with a blue ribbon in her hair, ran up to him and asked: 'Are you hurt, Cillian, are you hurt?' Her cheeks were red from crying. She wore one saffron sandal and one blue.

'No, no, I'm fine. We'll be back again next year. Don't worry, sure you won't?' he said.

'I won't, Cillian. You're great, Cillian. I love you, Cillian.'

'I know you do. I know that. What's your name?'

'Saoirse, Cillian. Saoirse Keane.'

'Thanks for all your support, Saoirse. We'll be back again next year, don't worry.' He patted her on the shoulder and smiled.

At that, the girl burst into tears and hugged him, her head banging into his ribs. Her mother had to peel her off.

Shallow breaths.

The mother, a dark-haired woman he thought he knew, smiled at him and nodded. The pity in her eyes enraged him. He shuffled to the bus and cast his bag and hurleys into the luggage compartment. He had forgotten to tape the hurleys together and they clattered and slid along the smooth surface.

No sign of him. Better to get it over with, but not in front of other people.

He thought about the time his father had hit him, after he gave cheek at his Confirmation. It wasn't a clean shot, but the shock of it stunned him – he'd never been punched before. He remembered being frozen rigid in terror as he lay on the ground, staring up at the towering figure above him.

'*What* did you just say?' his father had hissed through gritted teeth. Overcome by fear, McMahon had jumped up and run away. Why he went to the Clearys' house he never really knew, but he had been glad of the kindness and sympathy. He could vividly remember that small kitchen, and he, sitting there in his good clothes, crying like a baby, while Mrs Cleary wiped his nose, tried to calm him down and get him to eat a biscuit.

His mother picked him up half-an-hour later in tight-lipped silence. Took *his* side, of course. *Could she ever, just once, stand up to him?*

He flopped into the bus seat, put his back against the window and lifted his two feet off the floor.

That mad bitch Chloe in Galway. Twelve, no, thirteen. The American, Tara, fourteen. Only head, but still, she was a model so have to count her. His mind drifted back to the game. He closed his eyes, and fought against the images. Michelle, that married one from Cloghroe. She did half the team, but she was a good ride, in fairness. Fifteen. There was at least one more, but he couldn't remember.

The bus edged out of the huge gate and away from the stadium. A group of Cork supporters jeered them as they passed.

Sully's scoring goals, he's scoring goals.

Oh to, oh to be, oh to be a Rebel!

Lose-ers, lose-ers, lose-ers.

Back pressed against the window, McMahon swallowed hard, his mouth dry. He had forgotten to bring a bottle with him, despite Jim warning them about rehydration.

He glanced to his right and saw Dave Hogan take a sip from an energy drink. Hogan, whom Ruth had invited to her Debs, and gotten off with a few times after the Leaving Cert. Hogan had been the first to have sex with her – McMahon had wheedled it out of her that night when she was high on Es in Vicar Street. She'd done it with some other guy too – she wouldn't say who – in first-year, before she was going out with him. He'd stormed out of the gig, she stumbling after him, whining. 'Cillian, Cillian, I'm sorry, I shouldn't have said. I'm sorry, Cillian, I'm sorry.' Staggering down Christchurch in her high heels. Hardly spoke to her the following day while she sniffled and whispered to her 'friend' Leah. Leah who hated him because he told her she was frigid when she would only give him a hand job that time Ruth had gone home for the weekend. Fucked Ruth's brains out that Sunday night too when she got back. She likes it rough.

He took his phone from his tracksuit pocket and looked at it. He almost turned it on to see his Twitter feed, to find out what his 48,000 followers were saying. Bound to be some support there, at least some people would appreciate what he's done for the county. He twirled the phone in his hand and licked his lips. He really needed some water. Maybe he should text his agent, Nick Connolly: he'd know what to post. Something apologetic, but about pride in the jersey too. *#betternextyear #wewillbeback.* Maybe something to remind them of all the scores he got in this year's championship: 1–2 in the first match against Cork, and probably the goal of the year; 1–6 against Offaly who'd played with a sweeper; seven points against Limerick *and* they double-marked him; 1–5 against Tipp including a goal in the last two minutes to win it; 1–4 against Waterford in the semi – no way would Clare even be in the final only for him. No fucking way.

And one point today. One point.

The bus pulled up at the hotel drop-off area and the players trundled out.

I am not *going to take any shit from him. Not this time.*

McMahon had to climb into the luggage compartment on his hands and knees to rescue his scattered hurleys. Nobody offered to help him either, the bastards. He wondered if he could get a punctured lung from one of the cracked ribs. When he stepped out onto the ground, he thought his feet might buckle under him.

Two lines of people on the hotel forecourt clapped the players as they trudged past. He saw his parents and Ruth among them. His father, in his good suit, head and shoulders above the other two, was stony-faced. His mother, in a stupid flowery dress, kneaded her hands in front of her. Ruth, her blonde hair highlighted by the Clare jersey, stood to one side.

McMahon walked forward, head bowed. He stopped in front of them. He tried to look up but couldn't. He felt his father's hand on his shoulder, and he was pulled into an embrace. The stubble of his father's chin grazed his forehead as he cried. His mother was upon him now too, her breasts pressed into his back. The pair enfolded him. Ruth stood to one side, her head bowed.

His mother made a strange shushing sound he had never heard before. He could smell that sickly sweet Fleur De Lys perfume she wore.

'I'm sorry,' he tried to say, but the words came out as a whine.

His father stood back. McMahon looked up and saw him glancing right and left at the crowd.

'Not your day, Cillian,' his father said, loudly, and patted him on the shoulder. 'Not your day. Stand up tall, now.'

McMahon took a deep breath, nodded and turned away to enter the hotel.

A few minutes later, sunk in a lobby sofa, he turned on his phone. He took a deep breath as an array of tones came through. He looked around for Nick. No sign of the fucker when he needed him most. He scrolled down his recent calls made and selected *Nick Connolly Agent*. He listened to it ring and go to Voicemail.

'Nick, where are you? I need to get a Tweet out but I'm not sure what to say.'

The text messages were mostly sympathetic and requests for interviews – fuck that, no way was he talking to the media, not even Clare FM. He didn't read the mail – he knew they would be from his Twitter feed, Cork people rubbing it in, or all those hater-losers who knew nothing about hurling. He looked at the symbol of the white bird on the blue background. His thumb twitched, hovering over it. He put the phone back in his pocket. James Clancy's father, John, came over to shake his hand and commiserate.

'Unlucky, Cillian – ye gave it everything,' he said.

'Thanks, John,' McMahon said. He leaned back into the sofa and closed his eyes.

He heard his father's adamant voice behind him.

'He was fucking useless, Dick, couldn't do one thing right.'

McMahon put his face in his hands, slumped forward and rocked his body, pressing his fingers into the bone around his eye sockets. The wild rushing in his ears was like the pounding of a storm. It blocked out all the noise in the lobby. He fisted his right hand and pushed his thumb into his ribs, right into the cartilage, until he could push no further.

Where the fuck is she with that key?

He rose and walked towards the hotel reception. Ruth and her sister Jessie were standing behind a pillar. Ruth held both her hands in the air and said: 'I can't, I just can't.' Jessie was trying to calm her.

'Can't what?' he said. 'Did you get the key?'

Ruth froze. She put her hand over her mouth. Her eyes were wild. Her nails were painted saffron and blue, every second one.

'Oh, nothing, Cillian,' Jessie said and smirked. She always did have the hots for him. 'Sister stuff.'

He walked to the lift and Ruth followed. He'd get it out of her later. He recalled what he'd heard his father say to Dick Lonergan in the hotel lobby and he closed his eyes. He leaned into the corner of the lift and banged his forehead against the wooden panelling. Ruth gazed at the door of the lift. She began to cry.

'Jesus, what is it, now?' he said.

'Nothing,' she mumbled. She stopped crying and wiped her cheeks. Her face hardened. McMahon glared at her – it was always about her.

Ruth fumbled with the key card at the door of their room before pushing it open. She held the door for him as he shuffled in and dropped his bag. She placed his hurleys against the wall and put her case on the ground by the wardrobe. They stood there in an awkward silence. Ruth rushed to the bathroom and closed the door.

Don't tell me she's getting her fucking period.

McMahon sidled up on the bed and groaned. For sure his ribs were cracked. He let his head sink down into the soft deep pillows. He looked at his phone again. Where the fuck was Nick? He scrolled through some of his Twitter feed – mostly abuse. He turned off the phone. He was exhausted.

Losers and haters, what do they know?

He looked down at his runners and imagined the bloodstains

on the white sports socks underneath. He wanted her to see them. He wanted them all to see his feet in ribbons. In fucking ribbons. He wondered if he should get her to take a photo of them for Instagram, but he could only do that if they'd won. He clenched his teeth. At least she would see them.

God, he was tired. So tired. He closed his eyes, letting the exhaustion take him.

Ruth comes back into the room.

'*Will you take off my runners and socks?*' *McMahon says.* '*I need to put powder on them. Doctor Jim said I have to. It's in my bag. And will you get me a drink of water?*'

She drops her Pandora bracelet on the glass table. She loves that stupid bracelet. She opens the side zip on his bag and takes out the tin of powder.

She kneels on the bed and undoes his laces. Her hands tremble, her nails are saffron and blue. Saffron and blue. She lifts his left leg by the calf and removes his runner. She does the same with the right leg. She unpeels a short sock, blotched red, and keens.

'*Oh Cillian. Oh God, oh God,*' *Ruth says, her eyes full of tears. She removes the other sock.*

He feels a deep satisfaction.

This is what I do for my county. This is what I do. For my county. They don't know. They haven't a fucking clue.

Ruth lifts his feet again, one by one, and puts a towel beneath them. She slides the ends of his tracksuit pants up to his shins. She twists the top of the tin and sprinkles the white powder out, concentrating hard. She shakes the tin up and down, her blonde hair waving, her breasts juddering. She shakes and shakes, and the powder falls like snow. It falls and falls. It gives off a faint antiseptic smell as it drifts down and covers his feet, his poor feet, in a high white mound.

She slides off the bed and puts the tin on the sideboard by the TV. She pours water from a complimentary bottle into a glass and puts it on the bedside locker. She sits in the armchair by the TV, gazes at him and waits to be called.

Good old Ruth, she does what she's told.

McMahon woke. Noelle! How could he have forgotten Noelle? The pair of tits on her. Sixteen. He knew it was sixteen, not bad for one year.

Bet you never pulled sixteen women in one year, you useless old dickhead.

He glanced to his right towards the armchair to beckon Ruth, but she wasn't there. The room had darkened and grown cool. The bathroom door was ajar, the light off. He raised his head and winced as the pain slashed through his chest.

He looked at his feet, throbbing now. His runners were still on. There was no glass of water on the bedside locker, no tin of powder on the sideboard and no bracelet on the glass table. Ruth's case was no longer beside the wardrobe.

'Ruth?' he said, his voice querulous and sharp.

There was no reply.

'Ruth?' he said again, more wistfully.

He slumped back on the pillows and clamped his eyes shut. The only sounds he could hear were his own untidy breathing and the hum of traffic in the distance.

A Pure Dote

Later, Nuala would wonder why it was always the bloody keys that Gerry kept losing. They ended up being found in the usual places – pockets or door-locks or the ignition. At first, she hadn't taken much notice of it; he was busy, they were all busy. So what if he'd become a bit forgetful, even at forty?

One evening, when he was going to a match, she saw him in the hall staring at the keys as if he didn't know what they were or what to do with them. It was then that alarm bells started ringing. She knew they were in big trouble on their way to Mrs O'Connell's funeral that wet Friday night in October. When he was driving through Buttevant and he asked her where they were going.

Oliver, the GP, was matter-of-fact.

'It isn't looking good, guys,' he said, and she had always hated that word 'guys' and the way people used it. People aren't 'guys'; she isn't a 'guy'. 'Don't call me a "guy", you asshole,' she wanted to shout in his face but, of course, she said nothing.

'But you never know. There could be a simple cause and if there is, the neurologist will find it,' he said, and he washed his hands of it. They never went back to him. What a cold fish for a doctor, a horrible man, and she doesn't say that often.

Neurologist. The word alone is frightening, drawing up an image of a brain in a dish. But Nuala realised quickly that fear was a luxury she could not afford, so she didn't countenance it.

Whatever about feeling it from time to time, he would never see it in her eyes, she decided – and he never did, either, and never will.

Oliver had not used the words, but the neurologist (a kindlier man than the GP, she had to admit – he had seemed sorry for what he was telling them) didn't hesitate in that cold office in Bishopstown.

Early onset dementia. Early. Onset. Dementia.

And that was that.

'Sticks and stones may break my bones but words will never hurt me?' Try telling that to someone diagnosed with early onset dementia in the prime of his life, with a wife and three young kids and a mortgage. Try telling it to his wife and children, his friends and family. Then you'll know what hurt is. Nuala knew what hurt was. Hurt was the love of your life turning into a helpless child, so that you have to look after him every day and sleep beside him every night and feed him and wash him and change his nappies day in and day out – the fine man you gave your heart and soul and body to – now a statue, a nothing, a mockery. Hurt was watching your children grow up without a father, but having to care for a shadow of a man who should be caring for them. Hurt was having to fight and fight and fight with strangers, day-in and day-out, for every entitlement, every support, waiting on phone lines, standing in queues, filling out online forms, swallowing the shame of the hand-outs she never in her life expected that she would be forced to accept. She would take the sticks and stones any day.

Oh, Gerry was brave, he was her brave man. His first fear was Huntington's and Pick's because they were hereditary and he was thinking about the children. When he had all those tests done and they were negative, he drew breath.

'I might be lucky,' he said one night in front of the fire. 'I might not have given it to them.'

She smiled. She hadn't felt lucky in a long time, but she knew she was and always would be. She took his hand and said, 'We'll face it together, all the way, boy.'

She sang a verse of that Johnny Cash song he liked, and he joined in. Later, they went upstairs and made love. In hindsight, she knew that was the night Jack was conceived, as sure as God. Sometimes you just know. Madness, of course, to have Jack when they did, but she wouldn't send him back and he the image of his lovely father.

The descent was rapid and spectacular, if that's the right word – she didn't even think about it any more, what was the point? It had been one last after another: the last day at work, the last time he drove, the last time they made love, the last day he fed himself, the last match he went to, the last time he spoke, the last time he laughed, the last time he went out, the last time he acknowledged her, the last time he smiled. Now there are no more lasts, are there? And won't be, until the last last.

The last time he smiled was the worst because it was the final expression he ever showed. Now he was trapped in there somewhere, thinking something, feeling something – nobody knew what, nobody could tell them. To herself, she called it his 'white room'. She imagined him in a room full of white light, so bright that there was nothing else visible – no walls, no ceiling, not even a floor. It didn't hurt, there was no distress, there was no past, no future, no other people – nothing but the pure white light. She didn't know where she got the idea from, a film maybe.

They used to have a joke and it was to that joke that he gave her his last few smiles. It was a dirty joke she could only tell him when they were alone, when the kids were gone to bed. One night she wanted a smile out of him so she sat down and told him, as usual:

Two deaf people get married. After several nights of fumbling around and misunderstandings in bed in the dark, the wife decides to find a way for them to communicate. 'Honey,' she signs, 'why don't we agree on some simple signals? So, at night, if you want to have sex with me, reach over and squeeze my left breast once. If you don't want to have sex, reach over and squeeze my right breast once.' The husband thinks this is a great idea and signs back to his wife, 'Great idea, so if YOU want to have sex with ME, reach over and pull on my penis once. If you don't want to have sex, reach over and pull on my penis ... fifty times!'

She finished the joke with a flourish, but there was no smile. Gerry just looked at the television, looked at her and then turned back to the television. Nothing.

Nothing is the worst; there are no words for nothing.

It was hard on the kids, too, though Caoimhe and Jack escaped the full brunt of it being so young – to them, in a way, their father was like an old beloved family pet with whom they have to be patient and speak to now and again and kiss goodnight. Nuala had seen Caoimhe grow tired of that role, lately, and she would have to say something to her before long.

It was hardest on William, she knew that. At eighteen, he

was old enough to remember his father in his prime and all the things they used to do together. Aisling, her eldest, her rock, was a pleaser and just wanted to help as often and as much as she could. She missed her daddy, that was for sure, but shaving him or feeding him brought her close to him and she felt better for having done him some good. For William, those acts were abominable, unnatural, and he hated the idea of them and he hated doing them and then he hated himself for his feelings. The resentment grew and grew until he broke down one night at Christmas the year before last, when she had him to herself, and she drew it out of him and he let it all go.

'It's not fair, it's not fair, I hate it,' he cried, wiping his eyes, sitting in the seat Nuala always associated with Gerry.

'It isn't, love. Not to your dad, not to me, not to you or Aisling, or Caoimhe or Jack. Or his own mother, poor Cassie,' she said. 'You know what, William, it's fucking shit.'

The shock drew him out of his misery and he laughed. So did she.

'Now,' she said, glancing at the clock, 'go out to the fridge and get a can for yourself and get the bottle of Baileys and a glass out of the press. We'll have a Christmas drink, just you and me. Not a word to the others.'

On that September Sunday, after Mass, she sat down in front of Gerry, but just to the side so he could still see the television. The All-Ireland was coming on. He watched sports for hours at a time, thanks be to God, not that anybody knew how much he could take in.

She combed her fingers though his hair, his lovely sandy-coloured hair that she loved to keep tidy with the sharp scissors she hid in the press and wouldn't let anybody else use. He watched the television. She looked into his eyes; was there movement there? She could never tell, but she was convinced he still knew her.

She smiled at him and kissed his cheek. Nobody took a blind bit of notice of her, they were all used to her by now. They had a crowd in the room, settling down for the match.

'Will we win, Gerry? I think we will,' she said. She thought about matches they had attended together in the early days, when they had just begun going out. Lord God, how her quiet man used to shout and roar at the hurlers and referee and then be all apologies to her afterwards. Sure she didn't care, as long as she was with him – he never said a cross word to her.

An hour later, while she was washing up in the kitchen, William came in, looking crestfallen.

'What's up, love, are we losing?'

'Yes, and we've run out of beer.'

'Why don't you pop down to Herlihy's and get some more?'

'I've had three cans, Mam, and I don't want to miss the end of the match.'

'Okay, love, I'll go down,' she said and took off her apron.

On the way home from the SuperValu with the beer, Nuala pulled into Meadowfield Terrace, where she had grown up. It looked tatty. Rubbish bins overflowed outside Brennans' and Dolans', and their front gardens were a disgrace. She parked at number twenty-one, her family's old house, where she had first made love to Gerry when she was seventeen and her parents had gone away for the weekend. He thought he was the whole man after that, and she thought she was a full-grown woman too. The world was filled with a new light making everything vivid and clear. It was 1986, the summer of 'Lady in Red', and they used to dance to it every Friday night in the Hi-B disco, their bodies moulded into each other's, French kissing.

She closed her eyes and listened – she could hear the song so clearly.

She pressed her head back against the headrest and felt the pain severing her in two.

'Oh, God,' she said, in a whimper. 'Oh, God.'

She wrenched at the steering wheel and squeezed it and pulled it until her arms hurt. She growled through clenched teeth and shouted: 'Fuck, fuck, fuck, fuck, fuck,' until something bubbled up inside her, making her dizzy and sick. She banged her head against the headrest and it felt good so she did it again, swinging back with more force each time, the thumping sound satisfying her, the pain in her neck satisfying her.

Later, weak and watery, she turned the bend into St Michael's Park for home. She hummed the little moon lullaby her mother used to sing her as a child. *I see the moon, the moon sees me.* Her lovely mam. God, she was a pure dote.

Nuala didn't care as long as she was with them.

'Every day is a miracle,' her dad used to say. Every day is a miracle.

As she approached the house and was about to pull in, Caoimhe jumped out onto the road, almost on top of the bonnet.

Nuala slammed on the brakes and Caoimhe, red-faced, ran around to her door. She lowered the window to admonish the child but Caoimhe shouted: 'Dad's smiling, Dad's smiling, Mam. Come in, come in.'

When she got out of the car, Jack ran to her. 'Dad's smiling, Dad's smiling. Cork won and Dad's smiling.'

She took his hand and walked through. Of the nine people in the room, Gerry alone was watching the television – all the others were looking at her or at him. Aisling was crying and William, Nuala could see, was just about keeping it in check.

And there, on her brown-eyed handsome man's face, was a blissful smile; not just in his lips but in his cheeks and his eyes and his forehead. The joy streamed out of her Gerry, taking years off him. Bringing him back to them.

She gasped and knelt beside him. 'Oh, Gerry,' she said, and he turned his face to her, the smile never wavering, and he saw her. He saw her. Then he turned back to the television, which showed grinning young men in red jerseys parade a cup around a huge stadium.

Caoimhe pulled at the sleeve of her blouse. 'Mam? Mam?' she said, pulling.

Nuala, unmoving, said: 'Yes, love?'

'Will Daddy get better now? Now that Cork won?'

Jolted, Nuala turned to her. 'Oh, no, love, no he won't get better, but isn't it lovely to see him smile again?'

She moved Jack and Caoimhe in front of her, put her arms around them and pressed the side of her face into Caoimhe's hair. Together they watched Gerry smiling.

His Frank O'Connor Moments

Dinny Young sat in companionable silence with his old friend and comrade-in-arms, Jimmy Mac, in what was pompously known as The Retiring Library. The way that hotels tried to evoke a grandiose home-from-home ambience would infuriate him, if he let it do so, but he didn't. On seeing that the scattering of books in the small room were of the touristy, *Quiet Man* type, he hadn't given them a second glance, but had sat down contentedly in the soft armchair and sipped his whiskey, glad of the morsel of peace.

Jimmy – big-boned and crooked from a lifetime of cycling, hurling and foresting in all weathers – nursed a pint of Guinness, which was set before him in patient attendance. He scrolled down through the social media on his phone and tut-tutted.

'I see Twitter is giving Cillian McMahon a hard time of it. Apparently he sent out some stupid tweet after the game. *#choker* and *#loser* are trending,' he said.

'None of those fuckers ever did a single thing for their county, you can be sure of that,' Dinny said.

'Still, it was amazing how bad he was.'

'It was. Sean was outstanding and Liam Óg too, but even so.'

'Do you think he was too cocky?'

'I don't know. Some of these fellas have a false kind of confidence. It felt like he was weighed down with expectations and he couldn't carry the burden. Thank God. There was no pressure on him last year and he just went for it.'

'Jack did a great job wing-back, too,' Jimmy said. 'Jesus, just as well.'

'Yeah. Dropping Paul S. was the hardest thing I had to do, all year. But I had to be ruthless and put down a marker after Dublin. Shake it up a bit. And Sean was the only man to mark McMahon.'

'They'd have had a field day if we lost.'

Dinny nodded.

'Do you really think he's not up to it?' Jimmy said.

'It was something Bill Barrett said when we went to see him. I knew what I had to do the minute he said it. Paul S. minds himself – too fond of himself by half. Finals are about the team, the collective, and not the individual. Anyway,' Dinny said, stroking the rim of the glass, 'it's done and dusted now.'

He let his thoughts drift to the moment he looked at Cillian McMahon in the Clare dressing room after the game and how he reminded him of his brother Michael, something in the blond fringe and the chin maybe. But not in the eyes. The eyes were those of his father at Michael's funeral, not looking outward but inward and emptied of everything except a scarifying bitterness.

Forty-four years ago, for God's sake – a lifetime. What kind of a person thinks about things like that at times like these?

But it didn't surprise him either – there *are* no revelations to be found – forget that shit. It's acceptance or nothing. That's just the way it is.

He still dreamed about Michael's drowning. When he'd wake up shouting and flailing his arms for dear life, Helen would shush him and put her hand on his cheek and say: 'It's okay, it's okay, Dinny. You were dreaming about poor Michael again.'

Poor Michael, his arm waving above the water, his head having dipped under it as the swirling current of the river carried him away. He'd fallen, his head hitting a branch on the way down, while the two brothers had revelled in the invulnerability of youth. They had been sword-fighting with sticks, playing Robin Hood on the big old oak bough that hung over the Bullworks by the Blackwater river near Mallow. Dinny had been the Sheriff of Nottingham that day, poor Michael was Robin Hood. Poor Michael, who will always be eight now, with his blond mop and his freckles and a smile forever showing a missing front tooth.

He turned to Jimmy.

'Did I tell you what Darren said to me after the match?' he said.

'No. What a great fellow he was, I suppose.'

'Ha! No. He told me that today was his last hurling match. He is heading off to the States in a couple of weeks, for good.'

'You're joking!' Jimmy said.

'No. I asked him about Na Piarsaigh and the county and he said he didn't care. He's off.'

'Hmm. Like a thing he'd do, too. What about yourself?'

'What about me?'

'You know what I'm talking about. Are you staying or going?'

Dinny rolled the glass in his hand and sipped the last of the whiskey.

'I honestly don't know, Jimmy. I'm tired now, but it might be different come January. I'm not going to think about it for a while, that's for sure. I'll need to talk to Helen too. I've neglected those girls and Lilly has her Leaving Cert next summer.'

'Fair enough. Well, you know where I stand on the issue. If you're game, so am I. I wouldn't say that now for anyone else. Himself is adamant he'll get two more years out of you.'

'Ah, well, that's Seamus.'

'He won't make it easy for you, if you do want to go, that's for sure. Same again?'

'It's my shout, I'll go.'

'You will not. If you go down there, they won't let you back up again.' Jimmy put away the phone in his jacket pocket, eased himself out of his armchair, tried to straighten up and shuffled out.

Dinny immediately closed his eyes and thought about his father, and what he would say to him tonight, if he had the chance. He wondered what his father would say back.

He relived the players' joy after the match, Sean Culloty's tearful speech in the dressing room. He thought about the knee ligament ruptures that ended his own career, the first one at twenty-eight, when he was at his peak. He wouldn't admit it for years, but he was never the same hurler again. He'd struggled on and on until Father Tom had to break the news one soft March evening that he was dropping him off the panel, that he just wasn't up to it any more.

He called them his Frank O'Connor moments. From the story 'Guests of the Nation' that Brother Hannon taught him in

Farranferris all those years ago, and that he teaches now to his Junior Certs. When the main character, an IRA man, after he had to take part in the senseless killing of a British soldier, says: *And anything that happened to me afterwards, I never felt the same about again.*

We all have them, even if we're not aware of them. At least that's what Dinny believed. Those existential moments in our lives, when we meet someone special, or when a beloved person dies on us, or goes away for good; when we witness something ineffable; when a child is born, or when everything we know is turned upside down by some titanic action or inaction – either through our own doing, or by fate's immutable hand. And afterwards nothing is ever the same again. We divide our whole lives into what we did and who we were before that moment and after it. Like a pivot, on which the stages of our lives hinge and turn, that moment when our understanding of ourselves and everything else on this God-forsaken planet is shot through with a kind of searing light so bright and penetrating that we can see right into it.

Was today one of those moments? He wasn't sure. He knew the previous ones – he thought about them often enough – but perhaps it was too soon to pass judgement on today's significance. Coaching Cork to an All-Ireland Senior Hurling Championship – the first for almost a decade – would surely rank high enough for most men, Dinny thought; but he was not most men, unfortunately. He accepted that, too.

The door burst open and six or seven of his team charged in, the captain Sean Culloty among them.

'Come quietly now, Coach, and there won't be any trouble. We're not taking no for an answer,' Sean said, with a pronounced slur. They were angling to carry him down the stairs, Dinny realised. Couldn't have that.

'Alright, alright, at least I've had an hour's break from ye. Jesus, what do ye want with me, anyway? Haven't ye anything better to be doing?'

A cheer rose up from the milling crowd when he appeared with the players at the top of the stairs. It took him an age to make his way through the well-wishers and back-slappers. He knew many of them. The selfies drove him cracked.

The foyer outside the Banquet Room was chock-full of people too, and the players dispersed among them. Dinny saw Helen's parents near the door. He wriggled his way to them.

'Jim, Betty,' he said. 'Great to see ye.'

Betty kissed him and patted his cheeks. She had vivid red lipstick on her teeth. Jim, his face flushed, gripped Dinny's hand in a vice and, weeping – he looked like he'd had a few – he said, 'We're so proud of you, Dinny, God we're so proud, boy.'

'Thanks, Jim, thanks very much. Why aren't ye inside?'

'We couldn't get in,' Betty said.

'Oh, for God's sake,' Dinny said, and they went inside past the County Board bouncers. Lilly, who was on the dance floor with Helen, ran to Jim and Betty to hug them. Holly, who was thirteen, was being minded by the parents of a friend, much to her chagrin.

'You escaped for a while with Jimmy,' Helen said, minutes later, as they danced to a slow Roy Orbison song.

'Not for long enough,' Dinny said. 'You'd want to see it out there – total mayhem. Some of the players dragged me back.'

'You're terrible, Dinny,' Helen said. 'Sure all people want to do is congratulate you.'

'I know, I know. I just wanted a few minutes of peace, to take it all in.'

She leaned up and kissed him on the lips.

'What'll I do with you, at all, Dinny Young?'

'I can think of a few things.'

'I'm sure you can,' Helen said. 'I think your daughter takes after you. What did she do only go over to Darren O'Sullivan and ask him out to dance.'

'She *what*?'

'Trooped over to his table and asked him to dance, the little rip, in front of everybody. Some Facebook Challenge, apparently.'

'Jesus Christ, that rubbish. I'll have to have words with her. What did he do?'

'He didn't know what to do. Coach's daughter and all that. His girlfriend saved the day, and they all went out on the floor.'

'Jesus, we'll have to watch her.'

'Don't I know,' Helen said. 'It's her Debs next summer. And then college.'

'Tell me, what did you get up to yourself, on your Debs?' Dinny smirked.

'Hmph,' Helen said. But a smile squeezed out of her.

'I don't remember you putting up much of a fight, either,' Dinny said.

'Anyway, that's exactly what I don't want her to be doing.'

Helen glanced across the dance floor.

'Maybe the Poor Clares would have her.'

'Jesus, it's not funny, Dinny. We'll have to sit down with her.'

'You'll have to sit down with her, I'm not doing it.'

'Coward,' Helen said.

'Now you have it,' Dinny said, and he looked down into her big blue eyes. 'Lady, the day I met you was the luckiest day of my life.'

'And don't you forget it, buster,' she said, smiling, and she kissed him again.

In the bedroom, just before 2 a.m., Holly phoned her mother in high dudgeon. Helen, who was about to get into the bed with Lilly, talked her down. Dinny sat on the side of the smaller, adjoining bed, listening to his voicemail. Lilly was sound asleep; she'd gone off the moment her head touched the pillow. Helen threw her eyes up at him and pointed to the phone. After she hung up, Dinny asked her what the problem was.

'Oh, she's just fed up she's missing out. Lilly passed on that Facebook Dance Challenge to herself and some others and she doesn't know what to do.'

'Jesus, what is it with that Facebook?'

'Ah, sure she hates to miss out. I'll go over to Dundrum in the morning and get her something,' Helen said. She switched out the light, lay on her back and snuggled down. 'Oh, and another thing. Apparently you'll have to introduce herself and Ciara to Darren O'Sullivan tomorrow night, they need their jerseys autographed.'

Dinny shook his head and sighed.

'Lovely,' he said.

'Kiss me, you fool,' Helen whispered.

He leaned across, kissed her deeply and sat back on his bed.

'Love you, boy,' she said in a faraway voice. She turned away from him.

'Love you, too, boy,' he said, and he looked across at the two forms in the bed, two neat breathing mounds, with two dark swathes of hair flowing out from under the covers. He pictured Holly in her bed in O'Keefes', hopefully with her phone turned off now. He set his alarm for 6.15 a.m. He would have to do more interviews in the morning with the radio stations.

He'd had enough of the voice messages – mostly media requests, however they got his number. He plugged the phone into the wall, put it on silent, turned off the light, slipped under the covers and rested his head back on the pillows. At times like this he wished he drank, really drank, so he could let loose and just conk out.

The first time his head goes under the water it's neither shocking nor distressing. He just lifts it above again, moves his long skinny arms and legs and begins to swim. His teacher, Brother Iggy, brings them swimming to the pool every Thursday, so he can already swim the breaststroke and the doggy paddle. He can nearly do freestyle, but he has to practise more. He learned how to float the very first day. You're a natural, lad, Brother Iggy said.

The shout is sharp and he turns towards it. Michael is being carried away on the current. Dinny swims downriver towards him, but the water is moving so fast. It takes him ages to reach Michael and when he does, he grabs a slippery arm and his brother turns to him.

'Help me, help me, Dinny,' Michael half-whispers. He is panicking, Dinny can tell, his eyes going way up in their sockets as he puffs and wheezes.

He is sinking.

Dinny feels the slap of a flailing hand and he feels a kick in his stomach. In shock, he lets go. He is gasping for air himself now, the kick winding and frightening him.

Michael disappears under the surface. The current drags him away, down to the pools where it's really dangerous and they are not allowed to go. Dinny is afraid and starts to cry. He treads water but the current has caught him too, so he turns and swims away towards the shore.

People are lined along the grassy bank. His mother and father and Granny Bridie and Grandad. Auntie Sheila and Uncle Dick and some people he doesn't know. Brother Iggy and some of his class. The Under 12 hurling team in their jerseys, all looking at him. He sees Helen and Lilly and Holly, with Sean Culloty and Darren O'Sullivan behind them, towering over them. He stands up in the shallow water. He walks towards them, crying and shivering, dripping water, his togs clinging to his bony thighs, his toes squelching down into the soft mud of the shore.

His father screams at him. 'Get in, get in, Dinny!' His father grabs him and pushes him back. His face is puce raw, misshapen in anger, spittle flowing from his mouth. He waves his hands. 'Get in, get in!'

'I can't, I can't,' Dinny sobs. 'I can't.'

'Get in, get in, Dinny,' his mother shouts. 'You have to save him.'

His father pushes him again and he falls into the water. It should be shallow but it isn't and his feet aren't on the ground any more. Now he can't swim either. Whatever he does, however much he moves his arms and legs, he's sinking down, down; his body won't stay afloat. He swallows a huge gulpful of water. He can't breathe. He can't breathe.

He felt arms around him. The sound of a familiar voice.

'It's okay, it's okay, Dinny. You were dreaming about poor Michael again.'

It was almost pitch dark, but he could see Helen's face, the crinkle around her eyes. She smiled at him and touched his cheek. He gasped for air, he sucked it into himself, lungfuls of it. His heart raced, hammering in his chest, like the heart of the stunned blackbird he'd picked up off the ground outside the window last winter.

'It's okay, love. You had a nightmare.'

'What happened? What's wrong?' he heard Lilly say from the other bed.

'Okay, okay. I'm okay,' he said and he sent Helen back to bed. The touch of her hand on his cheek.

He didn't feel okay, though. He could still see the disgust in his mother's and father's eyes, as they stood on the grassy bank, urging him to go back in the water and save Michael.

He dragged his mind away from it and back to his day. To those moments just before the final whistle, when it dawned on him that it was true, they had really won, it had happened. He felt again the surge of relief that had swept through him as the whistle blew and all hell broke loose. He smiled.

He knew now that it would be his last time – he would no longer be involved. It was over. He'd help Helen out around the house, give Lilly some grinds, do that MA he'd been promising himself, maybe go for a principalship – he should, the girls would be going to college soon.

It was enough; time to move on. He'd done his bit.

And did that change things? Did that make the win a Frank O'Connor moment? He thought again about his three sleeping women, two in the next bed and Holly in her friend's house in Douglas. He thought about the graves in St Gobnait's Cemetery in Mallow: Michael's and his parents'.

And he decided, yes, the final whistle today was a Frank O'Connor moment, and one that he would look back on for the rest of his life. Not because Cork won, but because it marked the end of his hurling days.

Maybe It Won't
Be So Bad

That N-Bomb didn't do notten for me, hardly no buzz at all. Waste of ten Euros. Only after making me fuckin' frazzled or something. All shaky, like. I hear someone running up behind me on the path but when I turn around there's nobody there.

It's getting dark, too. They're gonna be closing the park soon. Even all the Poles are after going home. There's still some kids in the playground so I'm not the last, but still. At least I have this seat, don't have to sit on the ground and get all wet.

The river, it isn't moving any more. It's like glass, like you could walk over it to them gardens on the other side. I wonder could I? Them big weeds by the water look weird, like there's something crawling around in there. Loads of maggots or something. It's probably just the wind, but still. There's a kind of squishy, sucking noise coming out of it. It's giving me goose bumps and I'm all itchy. Total rank, like.

Fuck him, anyway.

He knew I didn't want to.

'If you loved me you'd do it, Emma. It's only a ride, like,' he says to me the first time.

I goes: 'No fuckin' way.'

'It's only this once, I swear to God.'

When he copped on that wasn't working, he flipped, like. Then he was fuckin' *raging*.

'I told him you would, are you going to make a liar out of me? He's Patsy Coughlan's brother,' he says, leaning over me, grabbing me by the arm, pointing to the bedroom where yer man was waiting. His face all red, his eyes bulging out of his head. I knew he was going to hit me. I'd a desperate bruise on my arm, after.

So I done it. And it was mank.

If he loved me, he wouldn't make me. He owes them money. That's why he done it. I knew it wouldn't be the last time. The next time won't be either.

Then he gave me shit about it for ages. Did I come, did I like yer man doing it to me and all the rest. Shouting and roaring at me, all coked-up.

I think he might be after breaking my finger too; it's all bent. Hurts like fuck.

They'll all be wasted in the pub, celebrating the win. Full of it. Mam'll be shitfaced at home too, no point in going there 'til she's conked out.

If I could have one more, maybe just one of the small green ones, that'd get me down slow, like, later. I'll be okay again, tomorrow.

Something weird about that garden over there. Looks like there's people standing there, under the tree, staring over at me. In that other one too. I dunno, is that statue moving?

Nearly all the lights are on in them gaffs now. God, they're massive. Imagine having a garden that big, going all the way down to the river. They probably have servants and all. Imagine living in one of them – loaded, like, with Sully, having your own car and everything, maybe a swimming pool. I know Sully's not rich or notten, but what if he was?

I'd love to have gone today. Imagine going to the game with a real boyfriend. Somebody nice, like. Or with Sharon and Megan, maybe, and meeting Sully after the match, asking for his autograph or something and he brings me back to his hotel with the team. Oh. My. God.

Going to the match on the train, having a few cans like everyone else, and walking to the stadium. Couldn't be that far. Zoe and her brother done it for the semi-final. Tickets were, like, only €40 or something. Singing on Hill 16 with all the others, watching Sully score them goals and the whole thing. *Sully's scoring goals, he's scoring goals.* Singing all the way home on the train, out of it, having the laugh.

That'd be class.

'Darren Sull's only a bollox,' he says the other week when we were watching the semi-final on the telly. Darren blanked him on North Main Street and he's fucking savage over it. He probably looked for a sub off him, too. I seen him do that before. It's embarrassing; he has no shame.

Maybe it wouldn't be so bad in Auntie Karen's this time, she wouldn't be at me, like, constantly. None of her business, anyway, though if I was staying with her it would be, I suppose. I'll be eighteen in November; I can do what I want. Maybe if I went to London, I could get well away from him. Eddie could put me up 'til I found my own place. Might even let me stay full-time – he is my brother, like. Well, half-brother.

I could get a job somewhere nice, maybe. Lanzarote. In a pub or something and meet somebody nice. Somebody I could just get wrecked with, who didn't know what I done. Lie on the beach reading my magazines, getting a real tan. Not the fake shit, even though the stuff I robbed in Brown Thomas is the best ever.

I wish Nana Betty didn't die. I wish I was, like, ten again or something, and she was making me ham sandwiches for my tea and giving me tickles, and telling me stories, putting me to bed. Bringing me down to Madigan's to get lollipops and packets of sherbet and sticking the lollipops into the sherbet and licking it off. It's stupid I know but I can't help it.

At least I have my tattoo to remember her by. Fucking delighted now I got that done, even if it did cost me a fortune. Sharon says I should get one to match on my other arm but no way, like.

I'll have to go soon. I can't hear no kids no more. I'll wait 'til yer man comes to lock the gate. That guy on the bridge is standing there for ages and he was looking at me when he walked past.

Maybe it won't be so bad in the pub. Some of them might be gone home. His last Snapchat said he's after going back to the flat. Well, his last one before my phone died.

Maybe Roy will be around and I can get something off him. Roy is nice. Maybe I can just take a yoke with Roy, get a nice buzz on, have a couple of vodka and Cokes or something and then head off home. That'd be nice.

It's getting creepy. Doing my fuckin' head in. All them people over there and that sucking sound, and I keep thinking there's somebody behind me on the path.

There it is, coming out of the weeds, sliding on the grass, coming towards me. Slinking, like a snake or something, or a huge slug, fuckin' rotten, but I can't look away. I can't move; I'm, like, frozen solid. Somebody is in the garden across the river but I can't shout, I can't open my mouth. I can see more of them; there's thousands of them, all crawling over each other, making that sound. It's like slurping, like some oul fella with no teeth slurping soup or something. Sucking it up into his mouth. They're coming at me. Jesus fuck. I can feel my hands on the seat but I can't move them. They're getting closer but I can't do nothing. That slurping sound is getting louder. I can hear something else now; I think it's me, moaning. The first one is after reaching me. It's crawling up over my Superstars around to the heel, I can feel it. Jesus. Up under the back of my leggings and up my leg. It's wet and cold, all slimy and everything. The other ones are after reaching me now. They're crawling up too. My legs are shaking but I can't get up. I can't move or nothing. They're after going up under my leggings, up behind my knees and up the inside of my thighs. Some of them are outside my leggings; I can see them. They're getting faster. I can't move. Jesus God. They're crawling. Sliming. Up.

I jump off the seat and run around it and I feel my thighs and I hit them but there's nothing there, or at the back of my legs. I look at the ground and there's nothing there. I stamp my feet on the path. I'm panting, kind of whining, I can hear myself. I feel sick. I look at the big weeds and they're just weeds being blown by the wind. I look at the grass; there's nothing.

It still feels like there's something on my legs but I walk around a bit and press my hands against them, up and down, and the feeling goes away. I'm kind of shivering with the fright, shaking like a dog after getting wet, but I take a deep breath and get the bottle of Coke out of my bag and have a sip. I get my pouch but my hands are shaking so much I know I won't be able to roll up. I don't have no weed anyway.

I hear yer man with the keys walking along by the railings.

'We're closing up now,' he says.

I pick up my bag and walk to the gate. There's no one on the bridge. After going through the gate I just stand there. What if he's still in the pub? What if he was lying and he's there with one of them? I don't want to.

'Are y'alright, girl?' the man with the keys says.

I turn around.

'I'm not doing that no more,' I says to him. He looks at me stupid, from behind the gate. He has a roundy face with thick glasses and long black hair. He bends down to get a better look at me through the bars.

I start walking. It'll take me half an hour at least to get to my Auntie Karen's in Friar's Walk. My bag isn't heavy. I only have a few things in it since I took my hoodie out. My long T-shirt for bed. A toothbrush and toothpaste. The picture of me with Nana Betty in the small frame. My Tom Ford shades. My pouch of Amber Leaf, my lighter and my skins. My lip gloss and the good fake tan. A fold-up hairbrush. My iPhone and my Beats. Spare knickers and my Adidas leggings. My other Cork jersey, the new one with the Chill logo and the number 14 at the back. My purse with €40 and some change. A packet of tampons, a couple of hairbands and my phone charger.

Them railings look weird, like they're moving alongside me or something. I'll be okay when I get to the Western Road.

Alan and Maureen Dunlea are Awake

Alan Dunlea is awake.

He should be tired after his long, full day. At ease with the satisfaction of a win, somehow snatched out of nowhere. How, exactly, he isn't sure yet. He reaches for a simile. Comparing apparently unconnected concepts is one of the exercises in that book he bought five years ago, on his retirement: *How to Prevent Alzheimer's Disease with the Power of Your Mind*. What about: *Like clutching the flailing hand of a child who has fallen over the edge of a cliff?* No, too dramatic.

He remembers how the national anthem affected him before the match. He thinks it is the first time he cried since Billy's funeral. He knows why too. Alan Dunlea is no fool – it could well have been his last one.

It is quiet in the bedroom of his old house, Stella Maris, in his old estate, in Ballinlough. He can't hear any traffic from the South Link road. Good. Maureen is breathing easily, rhythmically, beside him. When she has a cold she snores. Or when she has had wine and cigarettes late in the evening, but that's rare these days. Since the diagnosis in March, they have both been abstemious (him from whiskey, she from wine). Not that they ever drank that much, anyway; although he used to worry about her when the boys were small, when she'd be on her own with them in Derrynane.

As if the Parkinson's wasn't enough, the subsequent blood tests showed high cholesterol levels, so he's also cut back on cheese and butter. Though Diarmuid said it's important not to lose weight, he is down three kilos. How could he not be? He wonders if he needs to go to the toilet again. All that water he has to drink with the Levodopa has him worn out from pissing. Maybe that's what's keeping him awake. But no, there's no need to go.

Dopamine. There's a pun there too, somewhere. That's another exercise – linking words. *That dope of mine.* No. *More dope for the dopamine.* No. *You're a dope without dopamine.* Almost.

It is still dark, still deep in the night. The glare of a neighbour's security halogen light invades the bedroom. That light is nothing less than a disgrace. He wonders if that's what woke him. He will definitely speak to Mrs Hegarty about it. Even if it were pointed downwards, but it comes straight in through the curtains.

It goes off again. Darkness is restored.

He twists and turns and lies on his back. A second pillow would be nice when he lies like this but when he turns on his side, one pillow is better. He presses his legs together to stop them moving.

His new friend, the resting tremor, whom he has nicknamed RT, starts up again. He'd forgotten that it's worse when he's on his back, so he turns on his side and thinks about the hurling. He imagines playing in an All-Ireland final. As Cork's full-back. The rock that Kilkenny attacks crash and founder on. Heroic catches in forests of hurleys. Mighty clearances high, high, way up into the forward line. Alan Dunlea and Billy Dunlea, the heroes of Cork.

Alan Dunlea is asleep.

Maureen Dunlea is awake.

Alan seems to be asleep. The tossing and turning has stopped for a while. And the tremor, thanks be to God.

Sarah, Conor's girlfriend, or partner, or whatever they call them these days, had been pleasant enough. A bit stand-offish, maybe. Maureen had thought that Conor wasn't serious about Sarah, but she's not so sure now.

It was awkward, meeting in the hotel like that, with Conor and Alan going off to the match afterwards. Not together, though. God forbid they would do anything together.

Why he brought *her* to the game instead of his father, especially given the diagnosis, God only knows. But he must have had his reasons. Thinks too much about things, does Conor. He's lost weight again, too – Sarah doesn't seem the cooking type.

Maureen thinks that she will probably never know what happened between Conor and his father, but she has her suspicions. The falling-out seemed to happen around the time of Alan's affair with that slut of a secretary. And she a married woman too, for God's sake. It must have been that. Conor must have found out, somehow. How stupid of Alan. When it came to sex, he hadn't ever been led by his brain, but by that thing of his. After Maureen found out about the first woman, Claire – if she was the first one – she had made it very clear that sex in the marriage bed wouldn't be on offer again. That was during her pregnancy with Anthony, so Conor would have been three. Twenty-six years ago now. Lord save us, where do they go?

She thought it would teach him a lesson, bigger fool she. To be honest it had been a relief not to be performing again those first six months. With Anthony so colicky and up most nights. And after the trouble she'd had with the birth. God, she thought she was going to die that day in the Erinville. It felt more like a bus was coming out of her, not a baby. An extra stitch for the husband, the doctor had joked, the cheek of him. Well, it was wasted.

The horrible memory comes back to her. When she'd eventually regretted her declaration and had grown frustrated. The night she'd relented, and made her move, and turned to Alan and stroked him. Her shock when he turned away. That little sound he made, almost like a snigger.

'Alan?' she'd said, half in hope, half in pleading.

'Go to sleep, Maureen,' he said.

And that was that.

She didn't speak to him for a month afterwards, but that wound down too. What was the point? A lot of people lived without sex. It wasn't as if she was going to walk out or anything; the boys needed a father as well as a mother. Later, when they were gone and living their own lives, she was too set in her ways to up sticks and start again. Anyway, the shame of it. No.

She remembers when poor Tom died what her friend Helen had told her about facing into a celibate future without him. That night Helen was drunk when Maureen had called over, about a month after the funeral. Apparently herself and Tom used to joke when they hadn't had sex for a while, and call each other

'Cobweb Mickey' and 'Fossil Fanny'. It took Maureen a while to get it, but then she did. She visualised her own vagina fossilising and hardening inside her, like a rock. A ridiculous notion, when you think about it, but it stayed with her, somehow.

Maybe Sarah had been nervous. That would explain her quietness, but it was more than that, too. She had a blank look, almost like she didn't understand, or didn't care. Maybe she's a bit dim, but surely not.

And that accent! God, what do they call it again? Plummy. That's it. She's a gorgeous-looking girl, no doubt about that, if it really matters so much. Maybe Conor takes after his father there, too. No. He couldn't.

Never gave her an ounce of trouble, Conor, growing up. Not once. Those lovely times in the house in Derrynane, when it was just her and the boys, who were hanging with tiredness and asleep at nine. Those everlasting summer evenings, with a book to look forward to, and the radio, and a glass of wine and a fag. Another long day on the strand to follow. Those long, sunny days, just tanning away and reading. So relaxing. Neverending.

Maureen Dunlea is asleep.

Alan Dunlea is awake.

He tries to match his breathing with Maureen's. He read somewhere once that if you do that, you'll get to sleep more easily. But it doesn't work.

How nervous she was this morning, before the meeting with Conor's girlfriend. Never shut up all the way up in the car. She was always fierce possessive about the boys – Conor especially.

It had been very good of Jim and Carole to bring them up to Dublin. That trip to IKEA was a fabrication, surely. A pity Jim has no interest in hurling. Rugby was always his thing in school and now it's all 'Munster this' and 'Munster that'. Carole is so like Maureen since she lost the weight. They're like twins, though Maureen is four years older. Or is it five?

A fine bit of stuff, Sarah, no doubt about that. Glowing, she was. The English have such poise, especially those upper-class women. God, that cut-glass accent. Reserved, but hard to blame her in the circumstances. If he were twenty years younger, he'd have given Conor a run for his money. Ten, even. Now, that's all over too, of course, along with everything else.

He turns on his back, then on to his right side, facing Maureen. He presses his legs together again.

Maureen said Conor wasn't that serious about Sarah. Never knew what he wanted at all, Conor. Never will. Feckless. He won't stay in that job either, no matter how well it pays.

Alan wonders if he had been too hard on the boys, growing up. But discipline is a critical element of any child's development – boys especially – and look how well they've both done. Yes, he didn't do many of the usual things with them, but a father's first role is to provide for his family and make his children self-sufficient and independent. Pampering never did anyone any good at all. That's just the way it is. Anyway, he could hardly get a look-in, with Maureen fussing over them all the bloody time.

The rows when Conor and Tony got older were bad. But he had to be firm. They had to learn who was boss. Now, it didn't help that things went so wrong between himself and Maureen.

Hard to justify those women, maybe, but life is for living too. If Maureen ever found out the full extent of it; those prostitutes in Dublin, and Carole that time, up against the wall in Lahinch. Ripped the knickers clean off her. God, that was a close call. The height of stupidity – with his wife's sister, of all people. But by God did she want a good fucking, too, and Alan Dunlea was the man to give it to her. Yes, life is for living. No regrets.

All water under the bridge now, anyway. They stuck the course and the lads are looked after.

He smiles when he thinks about the match again. What it must feel like, to win an All-Ireland. The final whistle, the cheering, the walk up the steps, the banquet and the trip home, the camaraderie, the open-top bus tour. The celebrations, the girls throwing themselves at you.

Alan Dunlea is asleep.

Maureen Dunlea is awake.

Saint Luke's Home is the best option. By far the best option, from the brochures she's seen and the visits she's made. Helen's mother is very happy there, and it's so convenient. When the tremors get too bad and he can't walk. Full-time care, there's no other way. They have physiotherapists, too.

It's just a matter of being practical, as he'd say himself. 'We are where we are, Maureen. Face facts. This is the situation we have to deal with, so deal with it we will.'

She thinks of the bridge games in Monkstown Golf Club. Tuesday mornings and Thursday afternoons. Lasagnes with wine from Marks and garlic bread. To be able to have a fag in peace. A new Fiesta, one of those automatic ones. Walks with Carole, she's always on to her since she lost all the weight. Netflix. Everybody has it except them; *he* won't hear of it. Some great series, Mary says, and you can watch the episodes one after the other, with no ads. Salsa dancing, maybe; Margaret said she'd do it with her.

It'll be hard for him to settle in the home, no doubt about that, but he'll get used to it in time. And they can medicate, if necessary. Money isn't an issue, his pension will still be coming in, and Conor and Anthony will help.

Long summer days in the house in Derrynane, when Conor and Sarah and their children will come to visit. Or maybe the children could come on their own, when they're a little older. She could get a Polish girl to help her, like the one the Murphys have. Gosia. Lovely little thing – she'll do anything she's asked. Maureen wonders if the Netflix will work on that old television in Derrynane.

The feeling of hope and anticipation on those summer drives down to Kerry. Of leaving everything behind. Through Macroom, on to Ballyvourney after the bends. Over the county bounds. On to Kilgarvan, Kenmare, Parknasilla, Sneem and Caherdaniel. Then that winding little road down into Derrynane. Such a lovely drive, into the setting sun.

Maureen Dunlea is asleep.

Alan Dunlea is awake.

There goes that bloody light again. For God's sake. He counts the seconds before it turns off. He doesn't need to open his eyes such is the glare. RT is going goodo. He turns on his side again. Fifteen. He presses his legs together to stop them from moving.

He sees a faint natural light in the room now. The dresser has taken form – it's nearing dawn.

Maureen is lucky that she can sleep so easily. The minute her head hits the pillow. If only he had it as good.

He recites the important terms he's learned off by heart from that book. *Dopamine: chemical substance in the brain that transmits impulses from nerve cell to nerve cell, regulating balance and … movement. Levodopa: drug which changes into dopamine in the brain. Dystonia: sustained muscle contractions and cramps that some people with Parkinson's experience. Restless leg syndrome (RLS): an irresistible need to move the legs and a frequent, no, a common cause of sleeplessness for people with Parkinson's. Antioxidant:*

Alan Dunlea is asleep.

Maureen Dunlea is awake.

He's asleep again. Could he not stay still for two minutes? All that tossing and turning. She was always lucky when it came to sleep, but now is probably a good time to move into the spare room. She's thought about it often enough, God knows.

He didn't react at all to the diagnosis – so typical of him. You'd swear the doctor told him he had a touch of flu. She was surprised he'd allowed her to go with him to the neurologist. Deep down he must have been worried. Sitting in the tatty old corridor in the South Infirmary for what seemed like hours. Frozen with the cold after the walk over from the City Hall car park. Which *he* insisted on, of course, because he still gets in there for free.

The words pouring out of the doctor's mouth and drifting away, like smoke. The only ones that registered were *Parkinson's*

Disease and *inevitable deterioration*. Why do they call it a disease, if it's not catching? She thought diseases were something that could spread, like smallpox, or AIDS, or tuberculosis.

He'd put on his work face, of course. She knows it well. The important public servant one. Principal Officer, Cork City Council. Rattled off questions to the doctor, Ó Mangán, or was it Ó Mahúna – some Irish name, anyway. He was a cold fish too, and well able for Alan.

The drive home in silence. She was more shocked than him, or maybe he just didn't want to show it. He always was too proud for his own good. He insisted on driving, of course. Then the rush to the Internet. The interrogation of what *exactly* the doctor had said. Only then did she realise why he had brought her with him in the first place – in case he didn't remember something, some detail. 'The devil is in the detail.' That's another favourite. Then the whiskey. Hard to blame him for that, in fairness, even if she had a desperate job that night getting him up the stairs to bed.

His head stuck in those books every minute of every day, since. As if reading medical books will help. Probably make things worse, if anything.

Hannah had always wanted to marry a doctor when they were in those digs together in Wellington Road. Must have been 1964 or 1965. All she ever talked about was doctors, before she met Jerome. Those North Infirmary dances she used to be dragged off to. Maureen had never seen the attraction – they were all so full of themselves. Ironic, when you look at who she ended up with.

They were great days, though. That lilac chiffon dress, and those pumps. That lovely lamé gold foldover clutch – you can't get them any more. Her first time, with Peadar. She had expected it to hurt more. She thought he was the one too, her head pressed against his shoulder to those slow waltzes in the Arcadia Ballroom. More fool, she. Once he got what he wanted, he lost all interest. Oh, what a beautiful dancer, though. Fred Astaire wasn't a patch on him. Waltzes and foxtrots. Two-steps. Didn't matter to Peadar. The feet of an angel. Waltzes and foxtrots. Two-steps.

Maureen Dunlea is asleep.

Alan Dunlea is awake.

He shudders when he thinks of the moment he knew Conor was behind him in the kitchen. That time, after his sixtieth birthday party, when they'd all come home and he'd had too much whiskey. Pressing himself up against Conor's girlfriend's bottom like that, as she washed some glasses at the sink.

She had started it, in fairness. Gave him the look at dinner. A saucy little bit. He was just about to put his arm around and cup her breast. She didn't resist, either. Pushed back against him, if anything. Pert little bottom.

That moment, when he knew that somebody was standing by the door. The shock on Conor's face, the rage, the coldness. The coldness ever since. Even this morning in the hotel. Even since the diagnosis. He wonders if Conor will soften in the end; you'd think he'd be over it by now.

No. It will ever be thus. That's a quote from somewhere. He tries to locate it, but it won't come. Shakespeare, maybe.

Antioxidant: an enzyme or alternative organic substance capable of counteracting the damage done, wait, *the damage done by the oxidation of the body. Bradykinesia: a slowness of movement. Dyskinesia: an involuntary movement, a disruptive side-effect of Parkinson's medication. Restless leg syndrome (RLS): the irresistible need to move the legs and ... and a common cause of sleeplessness for people with Parkinson's.* It is irresistible too.

Substantia nigra: a small part of the brain that degenerates. What a great word: degenerate. Alice used to call him that. Herself, too. 'We're an awful pair of degenerates,' she'd say, lighting up a fag, after they'd ridden the arses off each other in that little flat of hers in South Terrace. That shaky little bed – it's a wonder it didn't fall apart. Alice. The smirk of her, when he'd arrive to the door, half-cut and ready for action. *She* was always ready for action, the little minx. An awful shame she got that job in Dublin – she had been a great secretary, too. Plenty more where she came from, but Alice was one of a kind.

Alan Dunlea is asleep.

Maureen Dunlea is awake.

A terrible pity she didn't have more time with Sarah, to suss her out properly on her own. If only Conor had brought Alan to the match, instead of *her.* The two women could have gone shopping. Or sat in the hotel all day and had a nice lunch and a glass of wine. Gotten to know each other. Wouldn't be the first time she'd waited in a hotel lobby for Alan, but she wouldn't have minded today with somebody new to talk to. Conor's girlfriend – maybe his wife, someday, the mother of his children. They might even come back to Cork to raise a family; sure, London isn't a fit place for that at all.

And Sarah might make a good wife and mother too. Who's to know? So what if she has a posh English accent; sure we all have accents of one kind or another. Maureen remembers the slagging she got about her Stradbally accent when she first came to Cork. That little rip from Douglas, the manager's secretary. An accent is no reason to judge somebody.

Maureen hopes their first is a boy. Actually, two boys first and then a girl. Girls are hard work. She would have liked one, herself, after Anthony.

Not to be.

But the boys are so easy to manage. So, what's the word? Malleable. You can get around boys. Give them a ball or some rackets and they'll run around the strand all day hitting it. And swimming, and shouting, and feeding. Eat anything, boys. That's all they want. Running and swimming and shouting and eating on the strand. Grand.

Maureen Dunlea is asleep.

Alan Dunlea is awake.

No point in mulling it all over again. We are where we are. He'd known for months, long before Diarmuid eventually sent him to the neurologist. The handwriting, the dry eyes, the tremor, the change in his walk. Even Paddy had spotted his walk that day he called into City Hall to meet some of the old gang. Alan Dunlea is no fool.

The facial masking did throw him, though. The idea that he will recede behind an expressionless cold face, rigid and unmoving. What would be the point in living beyond that?

As if he were trapped behind a mask, like his father after the stroke. People walking around you and talking about you as if you weren't there.

God, the way that girl in the chemist looked at him when he chatted her up last week. As if he didn't even exist. That's what's happening; he's become invisible to them, something to pity. The same with Sarah yesterday, the shock in her eyes when she copped on.

It's all over.

Would he have the guts to kill himself before he gets too bad? He isn't sure. What defines 'too bad' anyway? When he can't walk any more? When he can't talk? Wipe his own arse? No, Alan Dunlea isn't afraid of dying.

In the meantime, he must get on to Johnny O'Sullivan, the builder, to renovate the sitting room into a bedroom, for when he can't manage the stairs. Shouldn't take too much, really. They like to make a big deal out of it, but he still has his marbles, they won't cod him. Fail to prepare, prepare to fail.

He'll miss the hurling, though. Days like today don't grow on trees.

God, those summers at wing-back, with Billy at corner-back behind him and Cash in goal. Nobody could get past that Rockies back line. Not even The Glen. Not even Ring. Those evenings on Church Road, training. Balmy evenings. Blue skies. He could run forever those days. Forever. Himself and Billy.

Alan Dunlea is asleep.

The Pride
of Kilbrittain

'The best match I ever saw Liam Óg play was that Under 21 semi-final against Na Piarsaigh,' Paddy Horgan says with authority to the others in the Skoda Octavia. He is glowing and giddy from the win. Clondalkin is dense with traffic, despite their quick getaway from the parking spot on the North Circular Road.

His pride when it was Liam Óg's turn to lift the cup. What an achievement for a small club like Kilbrittain and Liam Óg deserved the moment too, the way he had dedicated himself to his hurling. My God, how Liam Senior and Carmel must be feeling. He couldn't wait to see them, to congratulate them.

'Lord save us, he was only mighty that day,' Willie says from the back seat. 'Your man Sullivan didn't get a sniff of the ball.'

'He carried the whole team on his shoulders. I never saw leadership like it.'

'He played great today too. On McMahon as well, for most of it,' Donie says, checking his two side mirrors.

'He did,' Willie says.

'He never loses the cool. That's fierce important.'

'That's down to you, Paddy,' Willie says.

'What? Oh, Jesus, no. No, no, no.' He squirms in his seat.

'Indeed and it is,' Willie says. 'Weren't you drumming that

into him since he was ten? Didn't you train him at Under 12, 14, Minor, Under 21 and Intermediate? And for Carbery, too?'

'Ah, no, no. You either have it or you don't.'

'Paddy, today is your day too, boy,' Donie says, and taps him on the arm.

'I don't know. I did my bit, I suppose,' he says, the words stumbling from his mouth.

'Indeed and you did,' Willie says. 'And everybody in the parish knows it.'

Paddy looks out the window. He breathes slowly through his mouth, his lips pursed.

They are quiet for a long time after that.

Sheila met a man from Fermanagh shortly after she moved away, and they now have three children. They still live in London, near White Hart Lane, apparently. She sent him a lovely card when his mother died.

One day he bumped into her outside Kelly's Supermarket in Ballinspittle – she was pushing a buggy and had a small boy in tow. It was in August 1999.

'Hello, Sheila, it's Paddy.'

'God, Paddy, I know that, you don't have to introduce yourself.'

'How are you? And who's this young man?'

'This is Eoin. Say hello to Paddy, Eoin.'

'Hello,' the boy mumbled, in an English accent, squinting up at him.

'And who's this?' Paddy said, leaning into the buggy. A sleeping, angelic-looking baby was framed by the pale pink material inside. One chubby little hand clutched a plastic ring with some clowns attached. Her chest rose and fell, at what seemed like an alarming rate, under a white babygro with the smiling face of a tiger on its front.

'That's the boss, Anna. She rules the roost,' Sheila said. Her hair was different. Cut short, with a fringe. Jet black. It made her seem exotic. She had three earrings in her left ear. Her eyes were bright and she was tanned and fit-looking. She wore a tight black polo neck, although the day was warm, and jeans turned up at the bottom over bright red Doc Marten boots. She'd come into her own.

He pulled in his belly, which had been pressing against his tatty old jumper. He thought of his fine head of hair receding fast.

'She's lovely,' he said. 'How old is she?'

'Just turned nine months,' Sheila said.

'I don't know who Eoin is like. Tim, maybe?'

'Oh, he's more like his father's people. Don't do that, Eoin.'

She reached out and put her hand on Paddy's arm.

'Paddy, I was so sorry to hear about Denis. I only heard a while back. How is he?'

'He's fine, I'm sure. He's in Australia now. Well, I better be going.'

He was about to say he had somewhere to go, or somebody to meet, but the truth was that he didn't. He smiled at her and she smiled back. Eoin had picked up a small stick and was pushing it against the side of the buggy. Paddy got into the car and drove straight to The Cross Bar and drank twelve or thirteen pints and fell in a heap in the toilet and woke up at home, never finding out how he got there.

Paddy nods off on the Naas Road, despite his emotion. He wakes at the Portlaoise toll gate, embarrassed that he slept so long. He foosters in his pocket for some change.

'I have it here, Donie.'

'I have a Euro,' Willie says from the back.

Cora is sleeping. It's still bright, though there is a redness in the sky to their right, as the sun drops towards the west.

'Do you want to stop in Cahir or Cashel for a bite to eat, Donie?' Paddy asks as the car accelerates away from the toll gates. 'Or a cup of coffee?'

'I'm not sure. How are ye feeling?' Donie says.

'We're fine. Sure we're not driving. Are you okay, Willie?'

'I'm fine,' says Willie. 'Whatever the driver wants, now.'

'Yerra we might keep going so. Herself won't eat on the road anyway. Larry will surely do a sandwich for us when we get there,' Donie says.

'Oh, he will,' says Willie. 'Maybe even a burger. He'll replay *The Sunday Game* too, sure.' He rubs his hands together.

Looking after the minor teams was his favourite. The young lads were so eager to learn and to hurl, those days. They had some great players coming into their prime.

'Liam Óg O'Callaghan, what do you do if your man hits you a belt off the ball?' he asked one evening at training. A drizzle fell on them as they stood around in a circle after a tough session, preparing for the county final against Blackrock. He walked back and forth in the middle of the group, with a sliotar and hurley in either hand, his socks pulled up over the bottom of his pants. The boys were fit and healthy and keen and bursting with promise.

'I keep my cool and work harder,' Liam Óg said.

'That's right,' Paddy said.

'And John Long, what do you do when your man scores a goal on you?'

'I keep my cool and work harder.'

'You do. Okay, an easy jog on the spot, I don't want ye getting cold.

'Seamus Cahalane, what do you do after you score two goals?'

'I keep my cool and work harder.'

'You keep your cool and work harder.

'Larry Boyle, what do you do when the ref books you for something you didn't do?'

'I keep my cool and work harder.'

'Tony O'Sullivan, what's the most important ball?'

'The next ball.'

'Jerry Lynch, what do you do when your man spits in your eye?'

'I keep my cool and work harder.'

'Right. Remember that next Sunday. Whatever happens, and I mean whatever, you keep your cool and work harder. The next ball is the only ball. Two slow laps to wind down. Sean, put some ice on your face when you get home. Training again Thursday night, seven on the dot. Last man here does twenty press-ups.'

The boys dispersed to the sideline and began the jog, Liam

Óg leading them out. Paddy strolled towards his friend, Liam Senior, who was standing with two other men near the goal.

'Good session, Paddy?' one of the men said.

'Very good,' he replied. 'Great bunch of young fellas.'

It's dark when they pass the old house, derelict and shadowy behind the cypress trees. They are all wide awake now, nearly home. Willie has just finished a rendition of 'The Men of Beare'. How he remembers all the words, Paddy doesn't know.

After the water tank in the attic burst, he just moved out and left it there. No point in wasting good money after bad, sure the place had gone to the dogs. The kitchen was a complete mess and he didn't have the energy or the interest to do it up, with his mother and Denis gone. When he sold the twenty acres to J. P. Mulcahy, the Cork builder, for a housing development, he bought old Mrs Raftery's cottage at the bottom of the hill and renovated it. The work kept him busy all that year, which was just as well after he was laid off when Dairygold closed the Co-Op to build apartments.

It all belongs to NAMA now, of course, though he takes no pleasure in that. He's just glad he didn't have to get another job, but sometimes he thinks he might be better off if he did have something to occupy his time. The winter days are fierce long and the pull of The Cross Bar is often too strong to resist. Only for the dogs, he'd be banjaxed altogether.

He doesn't train teams any more after the young fellas began giving him cheek a few years ago. They were laughing at him behind his back so that was the end of that. No amount of cajoling by the chairman or anybody else could change his mind. He misses it sometimes, but what's done is done. It's a young man's game now, anyway.

He bought two apartments in Cork city and a small house in Ballincollig on the cheap and he rents them out, so that gets him on the road from time to time. He joined Bandon Golf Club, but it was hard on the old back, and a couple of women chased him off completely after they took a shine to him when he ended up playing in the mixed foursomes. He hasn't the heart to cancel his subscription, though it's money down the drain.

He thinks of Denis when they pass the pier. A few boats are moored nearby. The reflections of the lights from Courtmac across the bay glint on the water. He taught Denis to swim there, one summer, amid tears and snot and storming off and tantrums. He must have been only seven or eight, but he learned, eventually, and was like a fish after a few weeks. The little skinnymalinks, with his black hair and freckles.

He wonders if Denis ever thinks of him, when he's swimming on Bondi Beach or wherever he lives these days. He wonders if Denis is a husband by now. A father. That would make him an uncle. Sheila's lad, Eoin, is nineteen. Almost a man. He doesn't know if her third child is a boy or a girl.

The pub they are bound for will be hopping on the Sunday night of a Cork All-Ireland. It will be familiar and comfortable, full of friends and neighbours, celebrating the honour of the club having a player on the team. The porter will be creamy, and the replay of the match will be rousing. Larry will be fussing about his kingdom like an old hen around her farmyard.

After the pub, Donie drops him off at the cottage. They shake hands and arrange to meet up the following evening for the team's homecoming in Cork city.

The dogs bark as he approaches the house. The security light comes on. They jump up on him in welcome when he opens the garage door and he gives them a rub and lets them run around the yard.

He switches on the kitchen light, closes the door and fills the kettle. He walks down the hall and sits in his old armchair. The warm days bring out a smell in the living room, but he doesn't know what it is. Something gone off. He knows now that he won't sleep. He looks at the dark television and reaches for the remote. Something changes his mind. He glances at the drinks cabinet, but decides against it.

A breeze has picked up. He can feel the draught behind him, through the window that he's been meaning to fix. His mother's old clock ticks on the dusty mantelpiece. Yesterday's *Examiner* is scattered across the small table.

TJ scratches at the door and whines to get in – she's the home bird. Pooca would run around all night, barking at foxes, real or imagined.

He rises wearily from the armchair as the kettle comes to a boil and clicks off. The car keys are on the hook of the hall stand.

The dogs hop into the back of the Land Rover in a welter of sniffing and panting and wagging of tails. They are excited. They know their destination.

At the bend above Garretstown Strand, his car lights, just for a moment, sweep down over the foaming waves and he is glad that the tide is almost fully in. He pulls up in the usual place and lets the dogs out. They race off, the smell of rabbits and strange birds pulsing through the night air.

It's windy now, as it often is here. He walks to the wall and looks out into the dark sea. The night is overcast, not a hint of a moon or a star. The engine makes a slight ticking sound as it cools. A farmer has spread slurry that day, on the field beside the strand. A light in one of the houses up on the hill comes on and goes off. He hauls himself back up into the car. He is suddenly tired.

His phone, on the dash, buzzes with a text. From Liam Óg.

I kept my cool and worked harder.

Paddy Horgan smiles and types a reply.

You did. I'm proud of you.

He opens the window and listens. The sea seems quiet. The tide might have turned. There is only the faint sound of the waves on the sand, on the rocks beyond. He thinks he can see a hint of morning light to the east but surely it's too early.

He closes his eyes and listens as the waves gently flow and ebb, flow and ebb on the shore.

Can You Talk?

Two wine bottles stood on the table before Conor Dunlea – one empty and the other half-empty. He lifted the half-empty one to pour another glass, thought about it, and put it back down. The clock said 02:45 and he had work at 08:00. He flipped his passport over and over against his thigh – gold harp and gold writing on a purple cover. He opened it and studied the photograph again.

He looked out the window of his apartment, at the docked boats far below, faintly lit and indistinct in the mist. At Bermondsey Quays, restored, across the river; at Deptford further on, and Peckham beyond to the south. The lights of London City Airport were dimmed this late. He placed the passport on the table, picked up his phone and turned it on. He searched for a number in his contacts and pressed it. He listened to the American ringing tone until it was broken.

'Hello?' his brother Tony said.

'Tony? Tony? Can you talk?' Conor said quietly. Sarah was asleep in the next room and he didn't want to wake her. He didn't want her to hear this conversation, of all conversations.

'How's the going, boy? Jaysus, you're up late. Still celebrating?' Tony said. Conor could barely hear him with the din in the background. Tony was obviously in a bar. His accent lilted towards mid-Atlantic, a fact that irritated him when pointed out. A week at home in Cork cures him, but he reverts when he gets back to New York.

'Ha, now that you mention it. But not for the reason you think, actually.' Conor hesitated. 'I'm going to be a father.'

'What! Did I hear that right? Sarah's expecting?'

'Yeah, she just told me today.'

'Woah! Congratulations, bro. Conor, a dad! Jesus!'

'I know. Crazy isn't it?'

'How? I don't mean how, I mean: is it a surprise?'

'It was to me, anyway.'

'Oh.'

'Well, I thought she was on the pill. It wasn't planned, like.'

'Oh. Is there a problem?'

'I don't know. Maybe. It's just the timing. I wasn't,' he said, inhaling and exhaling, 'expecting it.'

'Right. Okay.'

'Can you talk now? It sounds a bit loud there,' Conor said.

'One minute and I'll ring you back. I'm in Molloy's; I'll just go outside. One minute.'

'Okay.'

Conor stood up, swayed for a moment, and walked carefully past the low armchairs and the green coffee table, his slippered feet silent on the thick pile. He checked that the bedroom door was closed as he passed and made his way into the kitchen. He leaned against a counter-top from where he could keep an eye on the door.

He looked back through the kitchen hatch. The wall-to-wall floor-to-ceiling Sherwood cabinets dominated the living room.

On their left, over the low bookshelves, hung the hand-signed Lichtenstein print *As I Opened Fire*.

He breathed slowly in and out, as Julie, his therapist, had taught him.

In: A new beginning; Out: A letting go.

In: A new beginning; Out: A setting free.

He turned on the tap, took a glass from the open cupboard and filled it. He took a long, slow drink. He felt his heart beat high up in his chest. It seemed as if it had been racing all day, before, during and after the match.

The phone rang and he answered it.

'Are you out with people?' he asked. 'You sure you can talk?'

'Jesus, of course I'm sure,' Tony said. 'This is a big deal, Conor. You're going to be a dad! Congratulations, boy. Hey, I'm going to be an uncle!'

'I know, I know. I still can't take it in. I don't know where to start,' Conor said.

'Well, how are ye getting on? Are ye okay? How was the match?' Tony said.

'The match was weird; she didn't know what to make of it. She was distracted half the time and I can see why, now.'

'Do you mind me asking why you brought her?'

'I'm not sure,' Conor said, gathering his thoughts. 'I just wanted her to see what it was like.' He heard the repeated clicking of a lighter and pictured Tony lighting up a cigarette. The sweet hit of that first pull of smoke.

'Well, hurling was always your thing. Uncle Billy made sure of that.'

Conor thought back to Billy's small house in Mahon, with its green and gold front door – The Rockies' colours. The feeling of ease there, chatting while his uncle read the *Echo*, fried sausages or weeded his potatoes, carrots and onions. In stark contrast to the unrelenting tension in his own home – the silences and the constant expectations, the spiteful comments and the power-base enforcing them.

He remembered his first All-Ireland final, in 1990, the year of the double, against Galway, and he only eight. Listening, rapt, to Billy's and his friends' stories in the car. The smell of the beer in the pubs. All the people packed so closely together in The Cusack. Billy holding his hand in the crowd. His mother fussing when he got home so late.

'Yeah, well, it was a crap match, not that it matters,' Conor said.

'Fuck, no, a win's a win. Sully did the biz, in fairness. Culloty too.'

'Yeah, he's some man. We were in right trouble until he turned it around. Where'd you watch it?'

'We went over to some dive bar in Brooklyn. Total kip, but it was a good laugh. How was Dad? Did ye meet them?'

'We did, yeah. He was fine. Lost a bit of weight, maybe.'

'And the Parkinson's?'

'About the same, I'd say. Not much wrong with him, he was chatting up Sarah at one stage.'

'You're joking.'

'Looked like it, anyway.'

'How did he get on at the match? With all the walking and everything,' Tony said.

'Fine, I'd say.'

'You didn't bring him?'

'No, no. I think he got a taxi. I wanted to walk.'

'Jesus, Conor, he's sick. You could have brought him,' Tony said.

'Why? Why the fuck should I? He never brought me, did he?'

'Alright, alright, calm down.'

'Yeah, sorry, but why should I? He never brought us anywhere, Tony. It was always Billy. Bringing us to matches, fishing, to the greyhounds. And Mam, bringing us down to Kerry. He was never around, and when he was–'

'Yeah, well, he was busy. He was working. He … I don't know. He probably did the best he could.'

'Did the best he could? You know what he put Mam through, you know about the women, about him trying it on with Cliona!'

'I know, I know all that but can't we just …' Tony's voice tailed off with a soft exhalation.

'Fuck's sake, Tony. You always take his side.'

'Jesus Christ, Conor, it's over, it's done with, right?'

Conor had slid down, his back against the kitchen presses, his fist pushed hard into his forehead, his elbows pressed against his thighs. He squeezed his eyes shut. He could hear his breaths come quick and harsh.

'Let's not do this again, Conor. Okay? Tonight, especially. Okay?'

'Okay,' Conor said, in a pained whisper. He stood and looked towards the bedroom. 'Alright. Alright.'

'Did he drive to Dublin?' Tony said.

'No. Carole and Jim drove them up.'

'Right. Hey, how did Mam get on with Sarah? Did she tell her all about the "lovely summers in Derrynane"?'

'She did, all right. Jesus, her and Derrynane,' Conor said.

Neither of them spoke for a time. Conor could hear the ambient sounds of a Manhattan sidewalk. There was live music playing nearby. Blues.

'Anyway, back to this baby,' Tony said. 'Mam is going to be delighted. She'll be over on the next plane. "Now, Sarah, you're to get plenty of rest and I'll cook dinner tonight. We'll have lasagne and some garlic bread and a glass of wine. Well, *you* won't be having any wine, obviously."'

'You're right. I'll hold off a month or two before I tell her; Sarah said the first twelve weeks are tricky, anyway.'

'Yeah, maybe just as well. How *is* Sarah, by the way? Is she okay about it? Is everything fine?'

'Yeah, yeah, she seems fine, she's only a few weeks gone. She's not sick or anything – yet, anyway. She's getting a scan during the week.'

His mouth was dry. He lifted the glass and drank some water.

'I just don't know what's going to happen,' he said.

'How do you mean?'

'I mean, I don't know if she's … I wasn't planning on getting married and all that.' He looked at the bedroom door. 'But I want to be there for the child. I don't want to leave my son or my daughter without a father – that's for fucking sure.'

'Course you don't, Conor. Course you don't. But that's not enough of a reason to get married, either. No way, boy.'

'I don't know, I have to think about it.'

'Yeah, but don't rush into anything. Play it by ear for a while. See how it goes. Give yourself a break too; this is a major surprise. A lot to take in, like.'

'Yeah. She told me at the final whistle. After we won.'

'Seriously?'

'Yeah, she just blurted it out, right there in the middle of the Premium section of the Hogan. But now I'm not so sure.'

'What do you mean?'

'It's like she had it planned or something.' Conor relived the moment: Sarah clutching her bag, her eyes wild and fearful as he moved to hold her. Almost yelping out the words: 'I'm pregnant.'

'Yeah.' He sighed. 'I think she did it deliberately, too. That she got pregnant on purpose. This isn't like her at all.'

'Hold on, hold on. What did she say? Why do you think that?'

'It's just, she's been on to me about settling down and moving in with me for a while. She's always complaining about her job, how she'd love to quit. I don't know.' He pushed his fingers and thumb against his forehead.

'Is that all? Sure women are always doing that. Jesus, I was only going out with Maria for a month and she was talking about weddings. Everybody complains about their job. Fuck's sake, I'd quit mine in the morning if I could afford it.'

'I know, I know, but I don't think I'm wrong about this. I dunno. And the funny thing is: I've just been offered a promotion in Shanghai, a partnership, heading up Asia-Pacific.'

'Fuck. What are you going to do?'

'I don't know.'

Conor walked back into the living room, poured more wine and sat on the sofa by the window. The reflection he saw in the glass was that of his father and he resented the likeness.

He took a deep breath and exhaled slowly. He bowed his head and closed his eyes.

'Conor? Are you there?'

'Yeah, yeah, I'm here.' He felt the teardrop on his lip before he knew he was crying. He put down the glass and wiped his cheeks. He sniffled.

'You okay, bro? You alright, boy? Conor?'

'Yeah, yeah, I'm fine. I was thinking of Billy,' Conor said. 'How much he'd have loved today.' He wiped his nose with the back of his hand.

'He would have,' Tony said.

'Anyway, the other thing is, I'm getting counselling. I think I'm suffering from depression. No, I *am* suffering from depression. So, I'm going to a psychotherapist,' Conor said. 'And a lot of stuff is coming up. She's working with me to be able to accept my past and open up.' He turned the wine glass on the table. 'Be present in the moment.'

'Is it doing you good?' Tony said. 'Do you feel better?'

'A bit. But I think it'll take a while.'

'Well, that's good. Sure half of New York are going to therapists. Must be something in it,' Tony said.

Conor thought about Billy again. In the Mercy Hospital, before he died. His raggedy striped pyjamas hanging off him like something out of Auschwitz. In the end, Conor had to read the match reports from the *Irish Examiner* to him, when the cancer took even the energy to lift the newspaper. Never a complaint or a bitter word. His only worry about his garden, his little garden.

His father hardly ever visiting his own fucking brother. All tears then at the funeral, chief mourner. *In … out. In … out.*

'What can you buy, when you cash in your store of resentments?' Julie had asked him. In that cosy little room in Chelsea where he emptied out his messed-up head in front of her. Four full days to his next appointment – that'll be a humdinger.

He heard the honking of a downtown cab over the phone. He had stood outside Molloy's many's the time with Tony, having a smoke and a laugh with the transvestites. That balmy New York city night air.

'You know what?' he said. Tony did not reply.

'If I had a choice between Billy getting cancer and Dad getting cancer, I'd have picked Dad.'

'Jesus Christ, Conor. Don't. Just don't. Go to bed now. We'll talk tomorrow.'

'Yeah, but why should we have to emigrate while he gets to stay at home?'

'We emigrated because there were no jobs.'

'We emigrated because of him, Tony. To get away from him as quick as we fucking could. Don't kid yourself, boy.'

'Jesus, Conor. I don't know.' Tony sighed. 'For fuck's sake, today of all days.'

Conor cleared his throat.

'Part of my therapy is to say to somebody that I love them,' he said. 'So, I love you, boy; I just wanted to say that.'

'I love you too, bro. Of course I do. A lot of people love you, you know.'

'I know. I often say their names out loud when I'm trying to go to sleep.'

'Oh, Conor.'

In: A new beginning; Out: A letting go.

In: A new beginning; Out: A setting free.

'Conor, can you ring that therapist at night? Could you ring her now?'

'No, no, I'm fine. I'm fine. I'll go to bed now.'

'And will you stop drinking? You're not on medication, are you?'

'No. No medication, thank God. Just the wine. Been a long day.' He sniffled. He laughed and said, 'I'm like a fucking baby.'

'That's okay too. Hey, we're not going to forget this All-Ireland, that's for sure.'

'Sully's scoring goals, he's scoring goals.'

'Yeah, Sully did the biz. You sure you're okay?'

'I am. I am. Just a bit wrecked.'

'Okay. You get some sleep, alright?' Tony said. 'What time do you get up? Will you text me when you get up?'

'I get up around 6:15. I'll text you then. I'm fine, honestly. I'm fine. Bye, Tony.'

He killed the connection. He glanced towards the bedroom door.

He picked up the passport again. He opened it – in that photo he always thought he looked more like Billy.

An image came to him. Of himself hand-in-hand with a

small boy approaching the Hogan Stand. The boy has fair hair and wears a red jersey. Standing on Jones' Road, fans streaming past them, the boy lifts his face up and says something. Conor bends down and answers. They walk towards the entrance.

He thought about weekends in Cork, bringing him home to matches to watch The Rockies and learn about his roots. Bringing him to Kerry, teaching him to swim. He'll surely get weekend custody and holiday rights.

He rose and put the passport into the bottom drawer of a chest beside the TV. He would explain things to Sir Richard at their one-to-one on Tuesday – that now was not the time for Shanghai.

He stood to his full height and moved towards the window. Right up to the glass, just far enough away that his breath didn't condense on it. He looked at his reflection in the window. He stood there, looking.

Ours

Sean parades the cup with his teammates around an emptying Croke Park. He looks into the thinned-out stand for a particular face. A tall man with grey hair. A narrow face. He is surprised at himself.

The relief is overwhelming – he didn't mess it up. He can't believe they actually won, but why is he thinking about that man now, of all times? And why was he thinking about him before the match too, in the dressing room?

He is nabbed by somebody from RTÉ to do an interview. When the interviewer mentions meeting Michael and Anne after the game he is suddenly emotional. The look in his dad's wet eyes when he was going to collect the cup. The feel of stubble on his cheek, the smell of whiskey from his breath. He knows he'll remember that touch, that smell, forever.

He does the sit-down press interview and answers the usual questions, saying as little as possible, as he had been trained to do by the PR people. He wants to shove it into them, to remind them that not one of them picked Cork to win today; it was going to be the Cillian McMahon show. But he holds back. They're not worth it.

His head hurts; he must get something from Doctor Ned.

One of the Croke Park ushers reminds him of Evelyn; she is small and pale in her purple waistcoat and skirt.

On the week before going back to school, into first class, Sean's father told him to come into the kitchen, that they wanted to have a talk with him. A talk. As he entered the kitchen, he tried to think of what he had done. He knew there was something very wrong when he saw his mother's face. It was all blotchy and red like the time of Granny Frances's funeral.

There was a ham sandwich and a glass of milk on the kitchen table. The crust of the bread had been cut off, the way he liked it. Normally his mother made him eat it. 'It will put hair on your chest.' He sat at the table but he couldn't take a bite of the food, nor a sup of the drink. He swallowed.

His father pulled out a chair and sat opposite him. His mother stood by the cooker, her arms folded, facing them. She was gripping a tea towel in her right hand. She had been drying up when he came in.

'Sean,' his father said, in a low voice. There was something like sadness in his eyes, and Sean thought there was going to be very bad news. The word cancer came to the forefront of his mind. His friend Seamus's mother died from cancer at Christmas and the idea had run wild inside his head ever since.

'You know about the facts of life now, how a baby is made,' Michael said. 'And you know what the word adoption means, don't you?'

'Yes,' Sean whispered.

'Well, Sean, your mother and I adopted you when you were a small baby. You see, we wanted to have children ourselves, to have someone to love and take care of, a little boy or girl. But, well, we couldn't, we couldn't have children ourselves, and the doctors tried everything but it wasn't possible. So,' he said, sighing. 'You know that we love you

very much and we always will. But we aren't your birth parents. We didn't have you ourselves. We ...' Michael looked at Anne, pleading, as if for help.

Sean stared at his father and burst into tears. His mother was upon him.

'We love you, Sean, you know that, don't you? Just as much as if you were our own flesh and blood. You're ours. You know that, don't you? You're ours,' she said.

'I do,' Sean sobbed into her breast. 'I do. I thought, I thought ...'

His father put his big hand on Sean's forearm and gave it a squeeze.

'It's okay, Sean. It's okay. What did you think?' Michael said.

'I thought one of you had cancer. I thought that's what you were going to say.'

Michael and Anne laughed.

'Cancer!' Michael said.

'It's not funny! Seamus's mam got cancer and died. It's not funny!'

His mother sat by his side. She put her arm around him.

'We know it isn't, love. We don't have cancer, we're both fine. We just wanted you to know about the adoption. In case you heard about it from somebody else. And we wanted you to know how much we love you and that we'd do anything for you. Anything at all.'

Sean cried again.

'I know, I know,' he said, blubbing. He picked up one of the sandwiches.

Michael and Anne looked at each other. Michael smiled palely. Anne's eyes filled with tears.

Sean scans the crowd in the high tunnel outside the dressing room when the team comes out to get on the bus, amid a frenzy of backslapping and hugging and selfies.

Would he really turn up, just like that? Or both of them? Now, of all times? That they would just be standing there, or walk up to him or something? And if they do, what will he say? What will he do?

The team boards the bus in the tunnel and he scrolls through the contacts on his phone. There it is, under T: Tim Collins. He had gotten it from Paul O'Neill, the physio, a few weeks before. He stares at it for a long time. It looks just like an ordinary phone number.

He ignores all the messages and WhatsApps and Tweets and texts and puts the phone back in his suit pocket when the bus leaves the tunnel under the Cusack Stand and moves through the dispersing crowd. He goes to the front of the bus, takes the cup off Jack Cashman and waves it to the fans who clap and smile.

Mick Crilly starts up 'The Banks' and they all join in. Sean passes the cup to Kevin Keane and sits back down.

He takes the phone out of his pocket again. He looks at the name and number. The bus picks up speed on the Ballybough Road, heading towards the river. He takes a deep breath and tries to think what he should say. Cork supporters cheer along the road, waving their red and white colours.

The lads sing 'Amore' now and Goggsie walks up and down the aisle, orchestrating. They're belting it out; even Jimmy Mac and Dinny Young are singing. Sean smiles and joins in.

After the Under 14 match in Caherlag, Michael drove Sean and his teammate Colm home. They had beaten their arch-rivals, Erin's Own, and the boys were ebullient, all chat, replaying the big moments in the game.

Michael dropped Colm to his house first. When he pulled into their own drive and switched off the engine, Sean opened the door to leave.

'Sean. Before we go in, I want to have a quick word with you,' Michael said.

Sean sidled back into his seat, the car door open. He looked down, ready for the rebuke. He must have done something in the match that he shouldn't have. But he couldn't think what. Maybe that solo run, when he lost the ball.

'Close the door there, like a good lad.'

Sean pulled the door closed. He stilled himself, ready.

'You've known for a good while now, Sean, that you're adopted.'

'Yeah?'

'Have you ever wondered who your birth parents are?'

'No. I dunno. Maybe.'

'Would you like to know, Sean?'

'I don't want to talk about this.'

'I know, Sean. I'm not too keen on it either but something has happened and you need to know about it.'

Sean looked straight ahead at the dashboard. His hurley and his bag were in his hands. He wanted to run away. But he knew his father would just wait for him to come home and tell him then. There was no escape.

Michael rubbed his hand over his mouth.

'Look, Sean. Your birth mother has approached us. She found out where you are, somehow, and she wants to talk to you. But it's completely up to you. It's your choice, completely. We feel you're too young, that you should wait until you're eighteen before meeting her, but we'll leave it up to you. Do you understand? Is that okay?'

'Yes,' Sean said. Michael had to lean forward to hear him.

'Yes, you want to meet her?' Michael said.

'No, no. I mean yes, I understand.'

'Oh. And? Do you? Do you want to meet her, Sean?'

In the team hotel there is bedlam. It takes Sean forty minutes to get past all the well-wishers to his room. He welcomes the few moments of peace and quiet with Aoife. It still hasn't sunk in.

He'd love a pint, but instead he lies on the bed while she takes a shower before changing. His phone is going ballistic, but after reading a few messages he's had enough.

He falls asleep. When he wakes up, Aoife, in her underwear, is rushing around the room. She sees him looking at his watch.

'It's easy for ye, all ye have to do is put on a suit,' she complains. She roots out a make-up bag from her suitcase and goes back into the bathroom.

He wonders if she would be up for a quickie, though his head really hurts and he's afraid he might have concussion.

His phone charges away on the bedside table. Buzzing on silent. He doesn't even look at it. He closes his eyes again.

Now would be a stupid time, don't even think about it. But he can't help himself, he does think about it. What will he say? 'Hello, this is Sean Culloty and I want to meet you'? It sounds stupid. What will Tim say? 'Yes'? 'No'? 'What do you want?'

He squeezes his eyes shut and presses his head back into the pillows. He puts his hands over his face. He hears a moan squeeze itself out from his closed mouth.

Sean took off his new coat. His mam had bought it in Leaders specially for that day. It was a stupid coat; he hated it. He realised that he was shaking, like he did when he had to read out loud in class. So he tried to think about something else. The time he scored a point to beat Glen Rovers in the Under 16 county semi-final in August.

The hotel was really hot when they entered. He had been afraid of puking in the car and now the nausea returned. There were people all around the lobby, a huge Christmas tree with red decorations in the corner. For a moment his mother looked lost. She stopped a passing staff member.

'I'm looking for the Duhallow Room, can you tell me where it is?' she said.

'Down the hall and up the stairs on the right. It's the first room on your right.'

Sean was definitely going to be sick. He tried to breathe through his mouth. Deep breaths, like he learned in training.

His mother stumbled in her new shoes, which she had given out about all the way from Glanmire. When they reached the room, she smiled at him and said: 'Are you okay, Sean? Do you still want to do this?'

He nodded, though he wasn't sure at all. He needed to know but maybe some other time. She took his hand and squeezed it. He let her hold it.

'You know how much your father and I love you, don't you, Sean?' she said. 'You're ours; you know that. Right?'

'Yes,' he said, and he thought he might cry.

'Okay, Mister Man,' she said, smiling. 'Let's do this.'

She took a deep breath and knocked, first meekly and then harder, on the door. Fiona, the social worker, opened it. She was flustered.

'Oh, it's yourselves; you're, em, a bit early.' She glanced behind her and sidled out into the corridor, closing the door.

'Hi, Sean. How are you? Everything okay?'

He nodded.

'Yes.'

'And do you still want to meet your natural mother?' Fiona said.

'Yes,' he said.

'Good. How are you, Anne?'

'I'm fine, Fiona, thanks. Before we go in I just want to clarify: you're going to be there all the time, yes?'

'Yes, absolutely. Because Sean is a minor I'll be there the whole time, unless you or Sean indicate otherwise.'

'And if we want to stop the meeting at any time, we can just leave?'

'At any time. You just say the word. Or you, Sean. And it's over. You're completely in charge. Is that okay?'

Fiona smiled at him. She was so nice to him, the way she explained everything. He could tell her anything and she would know what to do, what to say.

'Yes,' he said.

'Okay. Well, I'm just going to go inside for a minute and then I'll come back out and bring you in. Okay?'

There were no chairs in the corridor so they stood back and waited. He realised that he couldn't do it after all, that he had to get out, to get away. His hand was sweaty in his mother's. He had made a huge mistake. It was all a huge mistake.

'Mam,' he said, looking left and right for a way to escape.

Fiona opened the door and held it back. 'Come in,' she said.

Sean and Anne moved forward. He felt dizzy.

A small, sickly looking woman sat at the other side of a large table. There were bags under her eyes. She seemed younger and at the same time older than his mother. She was pale and thin. Very thin. She stood up when she saw him. She made a lonely sounding cry and held her hands to her mouth. Sean froze; Anne had to almost push him forward. Fiona said something but he couldn't hear her. He moved towards the woman, he didn't know how. He held out his hand. The woman held out her hand. It was bony and cold when he gripped it.

'Sean. Oh, Sean,' the woman said, in a strange tone of voice. He had to pull his hand away.

'Hello,' he said. There was a buzzing sound in his head. He moved back and stood still.

'You are so like your Uncle Johnny. Your father's brother. It's amazing. Oh my God,' the woman said, her eyes blazing. She had her two arms outstretched in a weird pose.

'My father,' he said.

'Your birth father, Sean,' Anne said. She put her hand on his shoulder and he turned to her. She looked frightened. He had never seen her frightened before. 'Michael is your father,' she said, and she smiled at him. 'Are you okay, Sean? Do you want to take a break?'

'Sit down, Sean,' Fiona said. 'It's okay. You're doing fine. Do you want a drink of water?'

'Yes, please,' he said, sitting down.

'Oh, Sean, it's so good to see you. I have so much to tell you,' the woman said. She sat down, slowly, on the edge of her seat, her eyes glued to him.

'Sean, this is Evelyn, your natural mother,' Fiona said, giving him a glass of water. Sean sipped it, and watched the woman.

'Sean, you have to know that we loved you from the moment you were born. If there was any way we could have kept you, we would have. Any way at all, but my father was terrible. He ...' she said and swallowed. 'We couldn't keep you, and, and Tim's father was sick and his mother wasn't able. I was only ...' Evelyn stopped talking and shook her head. 'Oh, I promised myself I wouldn't do this, but I'm so happy to see you.' Tears sprang from her eyes and flowed down her face, but she did not wipe them or look away from him. Sean felt like she was drinking him in. He was transfixed. He'd never seen anything like it, even at Grandad Mick's funeral. He noticed his mother was crying now too.

'Mam?' he said. 'Mam, are you okay?'

Anne wiped her eyes with a tissue and nodded.

'I'm fine, love. Are you okay? Do you want to keep going?'

He nodded.

'Sean,' Evelyn said. She leaned forward in her chair. 'You have to understand that we were very, very young when I became pregnant. Do you have any friends with sisters just a bit older than them?'

'Yes,' he said, thinking of Colm's older sister, Aoife, whom he really liked.

'Well, imagine one of them becoming pregnant. With no family support. My father was very strict and domineering. He threatened to throw me out of the house. Tim was only eighteen and his father was sick and in hospital. Oh, Sean, love. We wanted to keep you, we really really did.'

Sean watched her, willing himself to ask her. But he couldn't.

'Tim Collins. Your father is Tim Collins, Sean,' Evelyn said, quickly, as if reading his mind. 'He was a famous hurler, you might have heard of him.'

'Evelyn,' Fiona said.

Sean looked at his mother and she nodded and reached out to hold his hand.

'He would love to meet you, Sean. Oh, he would love to meet you so much. We don't have any other children, you see. We,' she held up her two hands, 'you did have a sister, Roisín, but she died when she was a small baby, she was very sick, she only lived for a few minutes. And now … Now, we're all alone.'

After the band finishes, the players begin a sing-song in the corner of the Banquet Room. Sean searches for Paul O'Neill. He has stopped drinking and immediately feels in control again. He had gotten a look from Dinny Young and he knew what it was about. He'll have to be fresh in the morning for more interviews and the visit to the Crumlin Children's Hospital.

The win is beginning to sink in and the lads are in mighty form. It actually happened.

He looks at the faces in the hotel lobby, scanning. He walks through the bar, but no sign. He'll have to let it go, he thinks.

He spots Paul sitting in a corner with a pint and a wide grin, chatting with Robbie O'Shea and Doctor Ned and a few others. Robbie is well on.

'Oh, here's the captain,' Robbie says. 'Looking for a rub-down, probably.'

Sean smiles and asks Paul for a quick word.

'I just wanted to say thanks again, Paul. Especially about that hamstring, Jesus, all the work you did.'

'No bother, Sean. You did the prehab, in fairness. I think that made all the difference.'

Sean nods. 'Hey, you know who I was looking for? Tim Collins, you didn't see him around, did you? I wanted a quick word.'

Sean's heart races again, though he tries to look nonchalant.

Paul purses his lips and shakes his head, a bit confused.

'Tim? No, no, I doubt if Tim is here. This wouldn't be his kind of thing at all,' he says, 'but he was coming up for the game all right. I heard that from Tony Murphy.'

'Was he?' Sean says, and nods. 'No bother. Thanks, Paul, I'll give him a shout tomorrow.'

He smiles, pats Paul on the shoulder and walks away.

Sean pushed through the crowd near the door of The Venue Bar with his friend Colm and Colm's father, Frank. Although only sixteen, he was already six feet tall and had a good view around him. Frank found a place at the counter and the boys asked him for Coke and crisps.

The sense of shock and anger in the pub was palpable. Cork fans, arriving in from the match in Páirc Uí Chaoimh, shook their heads and muttered to each other. Words like 'disgrace', 'shocking', 'desperate', 'woeful', 'have to go', were cast about with rigour in disgruntled tones.

A drunk man held forth at the corner of the counter.

'Not a clue, they haven't a fucking clue,' he shouted. 'Limerick? Fucking disgrace.'

He was tall and wore a black jacket and a white shirt that hung loose over his waist. He looked around and saw the two boys.

'Cm'ere, lads,' he said, slurring. 'No, no, no, no. No. Cm'ere. Cm'ere! I won't fuckin' bite ye.' He waved his hand in a beckoning motion. The boys tried to ignore him but they could not escape with the heaving mass behind them.

The man grabbed Sean's arm and pulled him closer. The man's breath smelled of beer and vomit and there was a dark crusty rim around his lips. His eyes were wet and rheumy. There was a coating of dandruff on his eyebrows. His face was flecked with stubble. Sean felt something shift inside him when he recognised the face.

The man leaned forward.

'D'you play hurling?' he asked Sean. 'D'you?' he asked Colm.

Sean nodded. 'Yes.' He leaned his head back, away from the smell, away from that man.

'Well, give it up. Waste of fuckin' time. Complete waste of fucking time. Give it up!' he shouted.

He released Sean's arm. The boys recoiled. The man took a gulp from his black pint.

'Hey, take it easy, Collins,' somebody at the bar said.

'Fuck off. C'mere, what did hurling ever do for us?' He laughed at his own joke.

Sean stared at him, mesmerised.

213

'What club are ye from?' the man said, swaying. He leaned forward and scrutinised Sean.

'Midleton,' Sean said, swallowing. He glanced at Colm. He could feel himself shaking. Something was churning in his stomach and his chest.

'Midleton? Midleton? Waste of fucking space. What? Listen here to me. Hurling? Pure useless. Give it up. See that load of shite down there today?' He pointed out towards the stadium. 'Limerick? Fuckin' joke. Not related to hurlers.'

Frank arrived with the drinks and pushed the boys forward. They found refuge out the back of the pub, in the beer garden.

'Jesus, the state of Tim Collins,' Frank said. 'That's terrible. And he was some player.' He took a sip from his pint and shook his head.

Sean held the bottle of Coke before him, his head bowed. He held the unopened packet of crisps in his other hand. Colm leaned into him.

'Why did you tell him we were from Midleton?' Colm asked.

'I just didn't want him to know,' Sean said.

Colm nodded. 'Want to go for a puck around later?'

'No. I think I'll go in home,' Sean said.

The baby in the hospital corridor looks at him, really looks at him, not a bother. The brightest blue eyes. Sean is shocked that the baby doesn't cry or something at this strange man picking him up. He's pudgy, pure white hair on his head, and a loose Cork jersey outside some bandages around his neck. A tube coming out of his nose is taped to his face and goes around under the back of his jersey.

'What's his name?' Sean asks the smiling young woman with tired eyes. He got the blond hair from her, anyway.

'Evan,' she says. She looks so young, he thinks. Couldn't be more than twenty-one.

'And how old is he?'

'He'll be two in November,' she says, grinning at the child.

'Not a bother on him,' Sean says. So she was eighteen or nineteen when she had him.

The other players stand around. Crilly puts a sliotar into the cup and holds it up in front of Evan and he sticks a chubby arm in to fetch it out. The cameras click and a photographer asks them all to line up and the baby gets a fright and begins to cry. His father soothes him and takes him and they all hunker down for photos.

Imagine giving away your baby to someone else, Sean thinks. To a complete stranger. All those sick babies and children, some of them probably won't even survive. But nobody gave any of them away. They wouldn't dream of it.

Sean tried to avoid the Avondhu coach after the game in Páirc Uí Rinn. He had been dreading the moment, win, lose or draw. They lost, and it was over before he knew it. Now he just wanted to get away from that man and that pitch.

But, heading through the gate, a hand was thrust out at him and the tall figure in the tracksuit said, 'Hard luck, Sean. You played well.'

He held the hand for a moment, barely glancing up. When he did, he saw a smiling grey-haired man, with kind eyes and a thin, worried-looking face. Sean moved on, towards the dressing room. He had to get away.

On the drive home, his father said: 'I noticed Tim Collins shaking hands with you.'

Sean nodded. 'Yeah.'

'What did he say?' Michael said.

'He said, "Hard luck, you played well."'

'Well, you did, Sean. Especially for your first Senior championship game.'

Sean nodded and looked out the window. They entered the tunnel.

'They say he doesn't drink any more,' Michael said.

Sean watched the concrete flashing by.

'He had that team in good shape, anyway,' Michael said.

'The two goals killed us,' Sean said.

'They did,' Michael said. He paused. 'Would you like to meet him, Sean? Properly, I mean? Now that he doesn't drink any more? Or Evelyn? You never met her again after that first time.'

'No,' Sean said. The car came out of the tunnel, into low evening sunlight. 'I don't know.'

It is eight days since the final and Sean has shaken hands with all the neighbours, signed all the jerseys and posed for the selfies and photos like he promised his mother. He has passed around the cup – they all had a go. It stands on the living room table now, appearing small and almost inconsequential. The Celtic engraving and old Irish writing are barely visible.

When Anne comes back from the kitchen with the tea there is a moment of quiet. A last cut of sunbeam shines through the window, painting an orange bar across the white wall, just behind the door. Sean looks at it, as he often did through the years, doing his homework or watching television. It narrows towards nothing, the end of just another day.

'I've a bit of news for ye,' he says. Anne's eyes widen. Sean laughs. 'No, not that, ye'll have to hold on another bit for that.'

He clears his throat.

'I've decided to contact Tim Collins. And Evelyn,' he says. He looks at his mother and father. 'If it's okay with ye.'

'It is, son,' Michael says. 'They must be very proud of you, too. I was thinking of them the day of the match.'

'When are you thinking of doing it?' his mother says. She has moved beside his father on the couch.

'I don't know. I have to drop the cup in to Tom Malone in Blackrock now. Maybe after that. Or tomorrow.'

'Evelyn will be delighted, Sean. It's a lovely thing to do,' Anne says. She looks worried and says, 'Are you sure?'

'I am. I've been thinking of it for a while.'

Sean nods and smiles at them. He begins to speak but stops. He looks at the ceiling and leaves out a long slow breath.

'Well, I better be going. Aoife will think I've been kidnapped or something,' he says, rising.

He kisses his mother. She pulls him to her for a long time and rubs his back with the palms of her hands. He swallows hard, leaning over her, and gazes at the arm of the sofa. He shakes hands with his father, then hugs him. A sudden sound erupts from his father almost like a laugh or a cough, but it isn't. Sean picks up the cup from the table and walks quickly through the door.

He parks in the lay-by across from Grandon's Garage. He takes out his phone. He thumbs the number. He closes his eyes as he holds the phone to his ear. It rings twice and a man answers.

A Study of Fandom in the Context of Darren O'Sullivan, Cork Hurler

I still don't even know what 'fandom' is. I should look it up, I suppose. Not that it matters. When Dinny Young phoned me last week and asked if I would talk to this girl who was friendly with his daughter about her Master's, I thought it would be something to do with physiotherapy, my field; or even something relating to pain, which is my speciality. More specifically, the perception of pain and its impact on performance.

Anyway, when Dinny Young asks for a favour, you just do it. I'd have met her anyway, even if I knew the subject beforehand, I suppose. I have a fair idea why she's studying Darren O'Sullivan, too. I'd better explain.

When Cork won the All-Ireland Hurling Championship for the first time in nine years – five years ago now – I was the physiotherapist for the team. So I knew all the players. And I knew Darren very well, because I'm from Na Piarsaigh, his club, too. We more or less grew up together. For those of you who don't know, that year Sully (let's call him Sully, that's what he's mostly known as) scored nine goals in five matches in the championship, including two in the final, and the song that was on all Cork hurling supporters' lips that summer was 'Sully's scoring goals, he's scoring goals'. I think it was taken from some soccer song, but I'm not sure, to be honest. Sully had a bit of a cult following at the time – hence the enquiries from the MA student, I suppose. It was the old story: men wanted to be him, women wanted to be with him. I guess it helps when you're six foot four and apparently look like 'a mix of a darker, younger Chris Hemsworth and a taller Adam Driver' – not my words. But there was more than that to Sully, too. A lot more.

I met her in Café Luna, which is just across the road from my clinic on Prosperity Square. It's a student haunt, which probably suited her, being near UCC, even if the coffees are a bit on the expensive side. It has a bookish feel, doubles as a second-hand bookshop, with large couches and little nooks and crannies. Nice place, good WiFi, lovely Portuguese tarts. I like to get out of the clinic, anyway, when I don't have a patient, to get a bit of headspace and look at the latest issue of *Sailing Today*. I was early and she spotted me straight away. I offered to buy her something but she wouldn't have any of it.

She was pretty, but not overly so: mid-length dark-brownish hair, medium height. I put her at twenty-three, a bit younger than I expected. Anyway, it looks like I was right: according to her Facebook page (I friended her straight away; it's still the best marketing tool out there) she is twenty-three. I'm very good on ages; I think it's a physio thing. She carried herself with a lot of confidence, I'll give her that. Very good posture, that's something

I noticed immediately – I'm sensitised to posture: it tells a lot. She wore oxblood Doc Marten boots and leggings (thin calves) but with a dress over them, and a small white denim jacket over that. Some part of her hair was tied up strangely in a knot, and she had a piercing under her bottom lip. Blue eyes. Nice eyes.

'Hi, I'm Emma,' she said, holding out a narrow hand (no rings) with some bangles at the wrist. I took it. I could see she had torn the extensor tendon of the distal phalanx of her index finger at some point, and it hadn't really healed. It looked like she had a tattoo going up her wrist, an N, an A and an N in ornate lettering, but I didn't get a proper look.

'Paul. Paul O'Neill,' I said. I stood up to shake hands, I'm old-fashioned that way.

She sat down and took out her phone.

'Do you mind if I record what we say? I'm crap at taking notes and I've a terrible memory.' She looked a bit embarrassed, her cheeks flushed. It was very attractive, I must say. I was taken with her from the get go, I know that now.

'Not at all,' I said.

'Did mister,' she said, shaking her head. 'Did Dinny tell you what my thesis is about?'

'Actually, no. Is it something to do with pain?'

'What?' she said, surprised. The scleras of her eyes were extraordinarily white – a sign of good health. They also accentuated the royal blue of her irises.

'Pain perception and its influence on performance; that's my main area of research,' I said.

'No, no. Oh, this is embarrassing. I'm doing an MA in

Sociology. I'm studying the phenomenon of fandom. Have you ever heard of it?' She turned her head slightly to the right when she asked this question.

'Eh, no,' I said. 'What is it?'

'Well, it's the study of fans. You know, music fans, sports fans, gamers and so on? Mainly the extreme kind. Those who group together? Harry Potter, Star Wars, CreatureX, that kind of thing.'

'Oh, right. So why did you want to talk to me?'

'Well, I'm looking at fandom in one specific case. In the context of Darren O'Sullivan by Cork hurling fans at the time. Although it wasn't just hurling fans. Or Cork people, according to my research.'

Now it was my turn to be astonished.

'Darren?' I said.

'Yeah, sorry. I thought you knew.' She squirmed in her seat. It was a nice squirm. She blushed again; it was a very nice blush.

'Oh. Well, in that case, I guess you have come to the right man,' I said in an even tone, though I was a bit miffed. I'd hoped I could impress her with my knowledge of the science (the very young science, in which I have five peer-reviewed papers published) of pain perception.

'Okay, thanks. I have a few questions I wrote down.' She pulled a well-thumbed spiral note-pad out of a battered old backpack that might have been white once.

'Fire away,' I said. Despite my disappointment I was also intrigued. An MA thesis on Sully. Well, well.

When people bring up Sully to me – and my clients still do (he's been a rich source of mystery and rumour since his 'disappearance'; every second year we keep hearing about a comeback – if only they knew), they are thinking of the grown man who got all the goals. That's who Emma was thinking about in the café. But I mostly think about Sully as a boy and what growing up with him was really like.

Hero worship doesn't come into it. He was a god, full stop. Whatever he did was the job. He wore brogues; the rest of us wore brogues. He switched to Docs; we all had Docs. He wore those long basketball shorts, so did we, even though they looked ridiculous on most of us – we weren't tall enough. He grew a 'tash at fourteen, so the whole lot of us made miserable efforts at 'tashes – his was perfect, of course, and the young ones loved it. He played for The Piarsaigh; we all played for The Piarsaigh – or tried to. He started going with a girl from Mount Mercy; we were all sniffing around the place, trying to chat up her friends.

The mystique wore off for me when I went to UL to study physiotherapy. I was a bit of a swot to him in the AG, a nerd, and that hurt, but I persevered – the degree was the best way of getting me out of St John's Park and I wanted that. Sully wanted to get out too, and maybe he thought the hurling would do it for him. I don't know, really, but I was glad of the distance by then – heading off to Limerick every September. I was glad when he fucked off to America too, though I wasn't about to tell Emma that any time soon.

'So, I'm not sure if you know that Sully had a kind of cult status that summer?' she asked, settling down to her task. There was a determined set in her mouth, and her forehead wrinkled up a bit, in concentration.

I nodded. If only she knew.

'Anyway, he generated a lot of online activity: fan fiction, discussion groups, hashtags, memes, blogs, GIFs, Facebook pages, and so on.'

'Fan fiction?' I said.

'Oh, yeah, that's people writing fiction online with characters from movies, or books, film stars or sports people. It's very typical fandom behaviour, especially among girls. It's mostly romantic.' She coughed. 'So, I'm wondering what you can tell me about Sully? Why do you think he generated so much attention?'

I stretched my arms behind my head.

'Jesus, where should I start? The goals? The good looks? The confidence? Not giving a shit?'

'Oh, oh,' she said, almost hopping up and down in her seat. 'Can you tell me about the confidence and not giving a shit?'

'You never met him?' I asked.

'No,' she said, and shook her head with a faraway expression that made me wonder if this was all personal. That made me jealous. Wouldn't have been the first time, when it came to Sully. Christ, there's Deirdre for starters. I sipped my coffee and thought about what I would and would not tell her.

Firstly I wasn't going to tell her the real reason for his cult status, if she hadn't already figured it out herself. It wasn't the goals or the looks – it was the disappearing act. Him packing in hurling after the final, not even finishing out the county with the club, heading off to the States just like that, *was* a shocker. At the very moment he'd reached his peak – All-Star, Player of the Year, nine goals, the All-Ireland – he was gone. That just didn't happen. Not a sign of him since, not a peep, just the odd newspaper article without a single direct quote. A lot of people think he's still in Chicago or New York.

When we learned that he was doing a runner on Deirdre because she was pregnant, it wasn't a big surprise. Not to me, anyway, or anybody who knew him. Me marrying her a couple of years later, when I got my own practice – that was a surprise. Considering I had been going out with her in the first place before she dumped me for Sully, and that I had to watch them together on all those team nights out and GAA functions, she all over him like a rash and me helpless to do anything about it.

I won't be sharing that information with Emma either.

'Well,' I said. 'Sully was one of those people who just didn't give a shit. But the more he didn't give a shit, the more things happened to him. For him. He didn't care about women, he really didn't – but they flocked to him. He didn't care about money, but he always had plenty. He didn't care about hurling either, genuinely he could take it or leave it – but he ended up winning an All-Ireland. He didn't like training – but he was as fit as a fiddle. He wasn't as good a hurler as Ray Clarke, he wasn't as dedicated as Sean Culloty, he wasn't as tough as Liam Óg O'Callaghan, but he still topped them all that year. He just had *it* – whatever *it* is.'

'And why do you think he stood out so much from the others?' she said. Here we go again. In reality he hadn't stood out so much from the others – except maybe to young women. Until he was gone, that is – *then* he stood out, all right.

'I'll tell you the main thing about Sully that year. He knew he was going to score goals and he knew we were going to win. I don't know how or why but he just knew. Did you ever see the film *Apocalypse Now?*'

'Eh, no.'

'Well, it's set in the Vietnam War and there's a famous character called Kilgore, played by Robert Duvall, and he's a colonel in the American army. He's a bit mad, afraid of nothing, wants to go surfing in the middle of a battle. The main character, Willard, played by Martin Sheen, says that the reason he could do crazy things was because he knew he was untouchable, he knew he was going to walk out of that war without so much as a scratch. He wasn't brave, or patriotic, he just knew.' I shrugged my shoulders and held her eyes and said, 'Sully knew too.'

She looked at me a bit funny. I'd given her something – I wasn't sure what, but she seemed to know.

She said something I wasn't expecting: 'Would you say it was destiny? *His* destiny, I mean?'

I paused.

'That's exactly what it was, Emma. Absolutely bang on. Put that in your thesis. And the destiny of the whole team hung on it too – the whole county. We shouldn't have won that All-Ireland, but we did. We were *meant* to win it. Sully was meant to win it for us – in the final, especially. So he did.' I drummed my forefinger on the table for emphasis.

Yes, Sully was meant to score goals and win an All-Ireland for Cork and I was meant to marry the girl with the kid he left behind. I don't think I've ever fully known why I married Deirdre and agreed to rear Sully's child. Maybe it was just because I could and she was desperate, or maybe I was glad to get his cast-offs. I don't know. Deirdre's sound out most of the time, unless she's in one of her moods. I could have done worse.

Truth is that they broke the mould with Sully. He's one of those people that leaves his mark on you. There's only a few people in your life that really, really make a difference in any meaningful way. I guess my father was one of them, and Dinny too. Pat, maybe, in UL. And, yes, the kids. But Sully's another one, and that's why Emma's chasing him down now and she never even met him.

I was a bit embarrassed by my 'destiny' speech in the café. It wasn't me – I was probably trying to show off. But when I looked at her for a reaction I could see I'd hit a nerve. She busied herself writing something down, even though she was recording the whole thing on her phone. She seemed to be writing for a long time and I didn't mind – I watched her as she did so. I decided to suss her out.

'Where are you from, Emma? Do you mind me asking?'

'The northside, just off Blarney Street.'

I nodded. That left a lot of scope, it went from Shandon Street, past Sundays Well, all the way up as far as Holyhill.

'Ever play camogie? The name is familiar,' I said – a blatant lie.

'God, no. I had more of a misspent youth,' she said. Which, of course, made me want to know about her even more.

'Oh, really?' I tried not to sound too eager.

'Well, in my teens. But I'm a strong believer in destiny. That what's meant to be will be. Do you know what I mean?' And she gave me a look I don't know how to describe, except to say it was charged with a kind of longing – what for, I have no idea.

I think that's when I fell for her. That's when I lost my safe mooring and ran adrift. I was caught in some current, and I still am, though I don't know where it will bring me. The anchor that kept me in place no longer holds any weight, any connection. I'm drifting. I may or may not land on the shore where Emma is. You never know with currents. But what I am sure of is this: it's taking me away from where I am now. Somewhere downstream – life is always downstream. Somewhere away from my 'happy' marriage with Deirdre and our two kids, Gavin and Chloe, my practice, and everything that ties me down. And you know what? I feel free. Frightened too, but free.

Truth is, and I've been lying awake thinking about this: I must have been close to upping sticks for a while, if this is all it took. It's not like I didn't have opportunities. Beautiful women come in to the practice all the time. Some serious athletes too – Jesus, the conditioning on some of those camogie players. My colleague Niamh made it perfectly clear a while back that she was available for some no-strings-attached extra-curricular fucking on the old therapy beds after-hours too, if I was interested. But I backed off. I'm glad now that I did.

Gavin is probably the reason Sully agreed to meet me last year when I was at that conference in San Diego. He did want to know how the kid was – he's not a total monster, and he has two of his own now with Kim, living the life.

I asked him if he ever missed hurling and he laughed, displaying perfect teeth – he'd had something done to them. He looked so American in that hotel lobby. With his confident slouch and his tan, his big smile and fine skin; his Tommy

Hilfiger polo shirt and his chinos and his tasselled brown shoes. He was meant for America and America was meant for him.

'I play golf down at the country club most days,' he said. 'Have a swim and a couple of drinks afterwards. Then Carlos drives me home.' He shrugged in an 'it's a tough life but somebody's got to do it' kind of way. 'It's usually seventy-five, maybe pushing eighty. Sunny. What do *you* think?'

I asked him why he never came home or visited Cork. Stupid question.

'Mam comes over a couple of times a year, we're working on a green card for her.'

Fact is, he doesn't need Cork; he never did. He knows he could rock on up outside the house in Grange in a big fuck-off jeep any time he wanted and give Deirdre another one. I wouldn't put it past him. And don't tell me she wouldn't drop her drawers at the very first opportunity with him too, or run off herself to California if he said the word. We both know it – I'm not totally fucking stupid.

I'll miss Gav – he's a great kid. Looks more like his mother than his father, thank God, but he worships the ground I walk on. I'll miss putting him to bed, and reading to Chloe, my one and only. Deirdre will go ballistic when she finds out what I'm up to – or when I tell her; I don't have a plan. She'll use Gav and Chloe to get back at me and squeeze me dry. I'm under no illusions about that and I can't say I won't deserve it. I hope I can still bring him out on the boat, Gav loves that, and I'll surely get some custody rights. But I know the way the courts treat fathers, too.

So, why am I even doing this? I'm not quite sure. It's not as if Emma's drop-dead gorgeous or anything. Or even that sexy, although I have been fantasising about those lips and that tongue.

She asked me a few more questions in the café, before leaving. Mainly about sociological issues to do with fame, reputation, group behaviour and leadership; I didn't even attempt to answer them – what do I know about that stuff? I told her she should talk to Dinny. Part of me wanted to drag out the conversation and keep her there, part of me wanted to process it, to take five and think about what was happening; so I let her go.

She never asked me about Sully leaving and I did wonder if she knew more than she was letting on. Dinny wouldn't have told her, but his daughter might have. I've met that girl, I can't remember her name – I guess she's not a girl any more, she's a woman too – and she's a bright spark.

After Emma left the café, I rang Niamh and told her to cancel my next client, that I didn't feel great. I ordered another coffee and tried to make sense of what had just happened. I rang Niamh again and told her I was taking the rest of the day off, and I headed up Barrack Street. As I was walking around The Lough fifteen or so minutes later, I had an idea. I stopped and just stared into the water. It was one of those light-bulb moments.

Maybe in the same way that I was glad of Sully's cast-offs, Emma would be too. Maybe I'm as close to Sully as she can get – in a way I'm another cast-off, we all are. Maybe that's really what she wants, so I could be in with a chance.

Yes, I had a lot more to tell her, but I held it all back. Even before she left the café, I already knew why. I wanted to meet her again, I wanted to look at those eyes, I wanted to hear *her* story, and I needed an excuse. Or maybe I didn't need an excuse – this is all a bit new to me.

And that's why I'm sitting here now in front of this laptop, looking at this email. Trying to click SEND. She gave me her email address – two addresses, in fact: one for UCC and one gmail. The gmail address is emmac14@gmail.com – I'm not sure what the '14' stands for. It doesn't matter; nothing does, really, except meeting her again, getting out of this drifting current and moving in the direction I want.

So.

Here we go:

Hi Emma,

Nice to meet you the other day and to hear about your very interesting thesis. Brought me right back, I can tell you. Actually I have a few other things about Sully you might like to hear about, if you're interested. Especially the whole destiny thing – I've been thinking about that. I forgot to tell you where he is now, and what he's up to.

I'm busy during the day this week and next – how about we meet in Tom Barry's some evening, after 6? Let me know what day suits. All are good for me except Thursday. You can get me on my mobile, which I already gave you, or you can message me on Facebook.

All the best,

Paul O'Neill

It'll have to do. I want to reel her in and I hope she'll take the bait to get as close as she can to Sully boy. But I don't want to sound desperate, either. She probably has a boyfriend, though it doesn't say so on Facebook. She accepted the friend request straight away. *And* she gave me those email addresses. I wonder, too, if I'm the one doing the fishing or if it's her. Only one way to find out, I guess.

Click the SEND button, you coward. Click it. Do it.

Why am I hesitating? Like I said, I'm frightened. Well, nervous, maybe. I'm giving up a lot. I know, I just know, that by moving the cursor over the button and by clicking that mouse, I'll be setting in motion a series of events over which I won't have much control. A lazy, drifting current can turn into a raging torrent pretty damn quick.

Fuck it.

Click.

The Glory
of That Day

Art is a strange desire. It was conceived inside me when I was eight years old, when I took part in a thing of splendour and immortality. It was an early conception and it has been a patient gestation. But now it longs to be out, to be freed. It is sweet but sharp. It is pitiless. It is hot and pulsing, piercing, prising, growing so that it can cut me open, ribbon my flesh, cast aside my blood. I can see my metal flowing out of me, placental, as in a messy birth. Streaming like hundreds of baby spiders out of an egg, into a webbed and dusty unknowing world. Into life. Into art.

Saoirse Keane knew she was seeing everything in London with new eyes. With ravenous eyes, gorging herself with as much as she could take in. Now that she was leaving in two weeks, maybe for good.

She glanced around the carriage at a typical Sunday morning Central Line scene: the usual array of multi-ethnic faces, everyone engrossed in maps or books or screens except for two chatting Sikhs, immaculate and proud.

She pulled at and smoothed down her jersey, the Banner saffron and blue. Her number, 15, proudly displayed on her chest and her back, the camogie crest on the right, the Clare crest on the left and the B.G.D. logo on the blue band below them.

It all sprang from that wonderful, terrible final, of course – fifteen years ago now – when Cillian McMahon flopped and she met him after the match, and he had been no less than a beautiful wounded Rubens' Saint Sebastian. Her poor mam had to console her all the way home in the car, and shush Shane because whenever she cried he did too. But she had been hooked.

After years of camogie with her beloved Sixmilebridge, she'd put on the saffron and blue of Clare herself on a sunny May day, in a minor match against Galway. The pride she'd felt when she ran onto the Cusack Park pitch with her band of sisters, all helmeted up for battle and glory.

The highlight, when she was eighteen, was being picked at corner-forward against Wexford in the Senior All-Ireland semi-final in Thurles, even if they were hammered out the gate. It was the last time, too. London was calling. Art was calling. But she still had the jersey and wore it on match days. She straightened her back, breathed deeply and tugged the material down.

The train pulled in to Marble Arch. She noticed a poster for The National Gallery: *Michelangelo and Sebastiano*. She'll go next week, though the installations at the Tate Modern are more her thing. Someday her work will stand in that great cavernous hall, too, and people will wonder. Someday. Maybe this MoMA prize will go on tour. Imagine, lil' ol' Saoirse Keane, the pride of The Bridge, commissioned by The Museum of Modern Art, New York city.

She still glowed with the memory of that *Observer* review of her first exhibition, after graduation. She knew it by heart: *Keane's gigantic pairs of figures, enmeshed and immersed in one another, as though locked in an eternal Olympian* agon, *rusted weapons and heads flowing out of Herculean torsos, like inverted Bourgeois spiders' legs – a triumph of scale and ambition.*

She would have her own *Maman* too, and those stuck-up New Yorkers knew it and wanted in on the show.

Her fingers tingled in her lap with the thought of it: the soft power of the pencil, sketching ideas, forms, pulling them out into the world. The immensity of the metal, its permanence, the fervid heat of the welder, that 'puff' sound it makes when, god-like, she ignites it. That white flame, the pieces coming together, freed into form. The elation when it begins to breathe itself into life, into the timelessness of the *Burghers* and the *Grandes Femmes*.

She tapped the screen of her iX3. Nothing. Carlos was still sulking about her not inviting him to Shane and Max's to watch the match. Well, not to watch the match, but to get a free lunch and lots of good claret – she should have kept her mouth shut about that. He wasn't the one either, but he'd do for now; with those hands and those big brown eyes and that fine strapping Catalan cock. But the moods! And the neediness. What's that Grandad Seamus used to say? 'God, give me strength.'

Why were they always so needy? Maybe the Americans would be different.

But it *was* great to see Shane so happy again, with loveable old Max to mammy him. Just what he'd needed after Colin did the dirt. Now they were living it up in their little Shoreditch pad, all prim and neat. She was just glad she didn't have to mammy him herself any more, the way she'd been doing since she was four and Shane was six and she'd flattened Tommy Ward, Traveller or not, for picking on him. But look, there it was. He was happy again, that was all that mattered, and he had Sky Sports on his TV, and Clare were back in the All-Ireland final.

She smiled, anticipating the lunch and the wine and the match, and her nerves, and screeching at the TV, and Shane and Max escaping with their dogs for a walk up and down Brick Lane to show each other off.

Two Kilkenny men boarded the train at Oxford Circus, sporting the black and amber. They saw her and grinned. One of them – tall and fair-haired with bright eyes – kissed the crest on his jersey ostentatiously. She smiled back. His hands were like something out of a Titian – enormous things, all bent and gnarled, a hurler's for sure. She'd have loved a closer look, but they always got the wrong idea when she asked to look at their hands. Well, sometimes it was the right idea.

The Kilkenny men got out at Chancery Lane and the tall one smirked and beckoned her to follow. She smiled again and shook her head. *We'll see who'll be smirking in a few hours, boy!*

At St Paul's she realised she'd cry whether Clare won or lost and when she'd see Cillian interviewed, as the manager; getting handsomer by the year, with his beard now greying at the edges. That first day when he came to give the training session to the camogie panel, she'd thought, child that she was, that he'd fall for her and leave his wife and they'd live happily ever after. The innocence. But she'd had other thoughts too, and she wondered if she could have made that happen. She told herself to forget about it. Half the girls in the county had a crush on him.

She'd known, even at sixteen, that she wanted out, that she had to get out. And that it had to be art. Only for all Miss Donnellan's support with the portfolio and her scholarship to Goldsmiths, who knew if she'd ever have made it. But she would have too, somehow.

Rigour got her to London and rigour kept her high, and here she was now on the Central Line, for her last time in who knows how long. Soon she'd be taking trains from Brooklyn to the studio in Long Island. No stopping now. No fucking way.

She had thought she'd be a painter, but in her first year at Goldsmiths, when the sculptor Karen Foster saw her sketches of figures, she said: 'Oh, my child, these are drawings for sculptures. They are so physical; I can feel them. They are hard, my dear. And so strong. Can you not feel them?'

So it was. Stainless steel at first, then cast iron and now her beloved bronze. When she walked among the *Burghers of Calais* on that class outing to Paris, the anguish of their hands ran through her like long knives. And when she stood under her first *Maman* at the Tate Modern, and then the one in Bilbao, she knew. Heart and soul, she knew.

She had been walking in a daze outside the Guggenheim in the rain by the river, in and around those spider's legs, again and again, looking, longing, sketching, touching, marvelling, until that Basque family had to drag her away to have dinner with them. They thought she was high on drugs, but it was something else.

As the train pulled into Liverpool Street Station, she rose to leave. She could feel the mounting sense of elation on the escalator, as it climbed up towards the iridescent light, all the people drifting by unseen, unheard, unknowing. That match, her first time in Croke Park. The anticipation for days beforehand, the early start, the long drive, the walk to the stadium, her little flag, her sleeveless top, her long flowing skirt. Her plastic sandals, saffron and blue. The saffron and blue streaming magnificently all around Croke Park. The red and white. Brilliant. Dazzling. Climbing up the interminable concrete steps of the Upper Cusack and emerging out into a delirium of possibility. The pitch flaunting its grandeur below, the stadium arraying itself around her. The thunderous noise, its expectancy like a weight pressing on her, and she pressing back. The sound, that sound when Clare came on to the pitch, the frenzied roar of tens of thousands; Shane putting his hands over his ears to block it out, and she adding to it, shrieking 'Up the Banner' like a banshee, waving her flag, as if something primal had been freed within her, released. She, only eight years old, but rapt with an ecstatic, blissful radiance as the teams paraded around the pitch behind the band. Aflame, aglow, like new starlight.

Cillian the last man in the line, number 10, with his lovely lime-green boots and his tanned legs and fair hair, his blue helmet in his hand, his faceguard glinting in the sun.

In that heartbeat the metal had materialised inside her, founding itself. Her metal began a knowing wait for its time, to breach her and to will itself into form with the fertile heat of the white fire that she had become. She knew this now; she thought about it and wrote about it often enough.

The straining of the hurlers that day, their exquisite power.

Their timeless grace. Their muscle, bone, sinew, blood, skin. The ruthlessness of them, the brutality, their cold will. Their hands clutching, opening, reaching.

And they calling to her, demanding her to reform them within her metal. All the hurlers of the past, the present, the future, calling.

Those thirty men – and she inside there with them all. At one with it all. The grass, the sky, her plastic seat, the high roof above them, the noise, her flag, her skirt, her top, her sandals, the light, the heat, the sound, that sound, her mother and father, her brother, the Clare fans, the Cork fans, the hurleys, the sliotar, the hurlers – oh, the hurlers, their hands, immortal.

The marvellous truth of it all.

The game drifting like a shadow into pain. The heartless, pitiless reality of it – that Clare could lose and Cillian fail.

Ah, but the glory of that day. The glory of it all.

The glory, soaring.

Acknowledgements

They say it takes a village to raise a child and a book isn't much different. My thanks to the *From The Well Anthology 2017* (*Smoke in the Rain and Other Short Stories*) and *The Honest Ulsterman* for previously publishing versions of 'Angels' and 'Fandom in The Context of Darren O'Sullivan, Cork Hurler' respectively.

Several people have read some or all of the book and I want to thank them. First of all, Mary Morrissy gave me invaluable guidance and support when I first put it together. Madeleine D'Arcy supervised my MA in Creative Writing dissertation in UCC – whence this book emerged – and she was a wonderful supervisor and mentor.

My writers' group have been great friends, advisors and supporters and they are an ongoing godsend. They are Anna Foley, Mark Kelleher and Eileen O'Donoghue.

Thomas McCarthy read an early draft and his inspiration and advice was invaluable.

Thank you so much to my other readers and advisors, including Ciara Coakley, David O'Callaghan, Declan Evans, Norma Coakley, Dermot Coakley, Colm Coakley, Úna Ní Cheallaigh, Mary Harrington, Billy O'Callaghan, Holly Cooney, Anna O'Herlihy, Mary O'Herlihy, Donna O'Leary, Adrian Connolly, Walter Wynne, Margaret von Mensenkampff, Armorel Manasseh, Niamh Kindlon, Mary Minnock, Martin O'Donovan and

Triona Ryan. Apologies if I've forgotten anyone.

Heartfelt thanks to all at Mercier Press: Sharon O'Donovan, Deirdre Roberts, Wendy Logue and Alice Coleman, but especially Mary Feehan, Patrick O'Donoghue and Noel O'Regan for their faith that hurling and literature could be a good match. Noel's sterling advice, encouragement and acute editing have been hugely beneficial to the work. Wendy's keen eye and attention to detail have also been a great help.

I want also to thank my lecturers in The School of English, UCC, during my MA in Creative Writing: Dr Eibhear Walshe, Professor Jools Gilson and especially Mary Morrissy, who taught me three fiction-related modules.

Thanks too to all my classmates and fellow-writers in UCC, for their critiquing, collegiality and friendship during the year: Beth Buchanan, Ed Cashman, Jenni DeBie, Robert Feeney, Anna Foley, Colm Furlong, Kathleen Hickson, Nicole Johnson, Alison Kavanagh, Mark Kelleher, Sam Lai, Rosi Lalor, Megs McHenry, Mira Mason-Reader, Julian Munoz, Una Ní Cheallaigh, Eileen O'Donoghue, Aoife O'Leary, Conor Roswell, Dominik Shultz, Nora Shychuk and Kelly Warburton.

Above all, love and gratitude to Ciara and my family, who have given me so much support down through the years.